Jack the Ripper Victims Series

Of Thimble and Threat

Alan M. Clark

More books in the Jack the Ripper Victims Series

Apologies to the Cat's Meat Man

Say Anything but Your Prayer

A Brutal Chill in August

The Prostitute's Price

Each novel in the series is a standalone story.
They are all available in paperback, ebook, and audiobook

Praise for the Jack the Ripper Victims Series

"*Of Thimble and Threat* is a terrifically absorbing read. A mature novel and superbly researched. The image of silver in the blood was woven expertly and made the ending luminous and poignant."
— Simon Clark, author of *Vampyrrhic* and *Night of the Triffids*

"Clark proves himself to be the ultimate double-threat, his prose every bit as evocative and compelling as his art. Steeped in Victoriana *Say Anything but Your Prayers* is a worthy edition to Ripperology."
— Steven Savile, author of *Silver* and *London Macabre*

From the review of *A Butal Chill in August* in *Ripperologist Magazine*:
Everything about this novel inspires admiration. It reveals terrible things about the world of London's poor, yet it is a work of great beauty, ceaselessly entertaining and compellingly readable. The rigging of a ship burning in the fire at the London Docks 'sparkles like a spider web dripping with dew at sunrise'. When we finally meet Jack the Ripper, he emerges from the darkness like an ordinary man, smelling of sulphur and soap. A Brutal Chill in August is a triumph.

From the review of *Apologies to the Cat's Meat Man* in *Ripperologist Magazine*:
Alan Clark is not the first author to find the victims' lives irresistible, but he has no equal when it comes to writing vivid and intellectually provocative stories about them. This is storytelling of the highest quality.

"In *Jack the Ripper Victim Series: The Double Event*, Clark's attention to details of the era reveals a class system where a poor woman alone is all but doomed to an early grave. Readers will come away touched by these profound portraits of desperate women and shocked by not just the crimes which ended in their demise, but the greater crimes of a society that offered them no hope. This book is a must-read; be prepared to be horrified."

— Nancy Kilpatrick
Author: The Power of the Blood series
Editor: *Danse Macabre* and *Expiration Date*

IFD Publishing
P.O. Box 40776
Eugene Oregon 97404
www. Ifdpublishing.com

ISBN: 978-0-9988466-5-1

Printed in the United States of America

Acknowledgments

Thanks to Cameron Pierce, Melody Kees Clark, Eric M. Witchey, Jill Bauman, Susan Stockell, Paul Groendes, Jerry Oltion, Jennifer Williams, Elizabeth Engstrom, Simon Clark, Troy Guinn and Pigg.

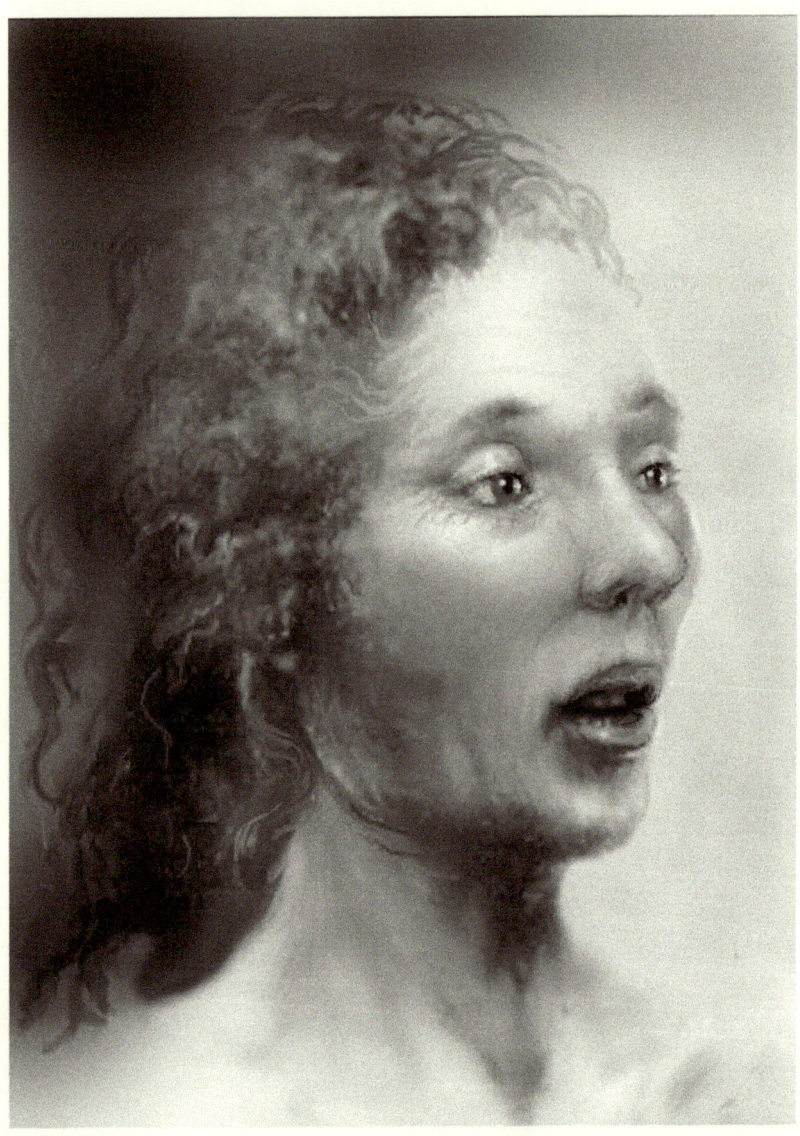

In an effort to bring to life an image of Catherine Eddowes, the author/illustrator digitally manipulated a mortuary photograph of the woman to arrive at the portrait above.

Author's Note

This is a work of fiction inspired by the life of Catherine Eddowes, a woman believed to be the fourth victim of Jack the Ripper. She also went by the name Kate. I refer to her in the story as Katie to distinguish her from her mother, who was also named Catherine. For purposes of storytelling, I have not adhered strictly to her history. I have assigned to my main character emotional characteristics and reactions that seem consistent with her life and circumstances. My goal is to provide a glimpse into a time when the industrial revolution had created not only prosperity, but also unimaginable suffering in what was the greatest city in the richest country in the world. Apparently it was a society in which the impoverished, and especially poor, single, middle-aged women were considered by many to have little worth. The murders of five women in the autumn of 1888 was only a symptom of the social ills in London.

Therefore, this is not the story of Jack the Ripper. If anything, the Whitechapel Murderer is merely a force of nature within the environment of the tale. It is the story of a human life tragically cut short, one that would have been quickly forgotten if the manner of her death had been anything other than astounding.

In modern times, information about those who are murdered is readily available. It flows easily and with little in the way of filters from the news. I am most often interested in what I can learn about what motivates those who kill. For my own emotional protection, I frequently shy away from thinking too much about the personalities, loves and aspirations of those who suffer from violent crimes.

My first real insight into the humanity of Catherine Eddowes came from reading the police report about her murder, particularly the part that listed her articles of clothing and the possessions found on her person at the time of her death. Catherine Eddowes had spent each of the two nights before the night of her death in a different casual ward. The casual wards were part of the workhouse system, a place for the transient, the ill, or those known to be criminals to receive temporary shelter in what was considered at the time to be appalling conditions. Like many of the homeless today, she was wearing many layers of clothing. She carried over fifty personal items. It is likely she had everything she owned on her person.

With a sense of what her time and circumstance were, I found this pitiful list more compelling than anything I've read about Jack the Ripper.

—Alan M. Clark
Eugene, Oregon

Jack the Ripper Victims Series

Of Thimble and Threat

Alan M. Clark

IFD

Publishing

Eugene, Oregon

A Thimble
Bermondsey, London 1855

Katie took the silver-plated thimble from the sewing kit on the table and palmed it to conceal it from her mother, Catherine. Once it was in the folds of cloth in her lap, she removed the old, dented black thimble from her finger and slipped on the silver one. If she kept her hands busy, Catherine might not notice. The metal, cool to the touch at first, warmed quickly and felt smooth and cozy on her finger.

After a lunch of half a potato, hunger still nagged at Katie. She would say nothing about it to save her mother's feelings, but her growling stomach said everything. As it became louder, Catherine smiled grimly. "You're a good girl," she said, "always so willing to help your mum."

Katie could distract with small talk too. "You've always worked too hard, but especially since Father died. If I didn't help, you'd work your fingers to the bone." She spoke with feigned sternness, tempered with a sweet smile. "And...I like having you all to myself."

Spending afternoons and evenings together was pleasant enough, sitting at the table, talking and mending the clothes Catherine's employer sent home with her each day; replacing buttons lost in the wash or stitching torn seams.

"I may work harder now, but what we have is worth the toil. We're more comfortable than we were in the attic room, and I don't have to walk so far."

Five years of walking to Bermondsey from their old room in South Bermondsey had taken its toll on her mother's feet. Laboring as a scourer, Catherine had been employed in this very room for those years. Visiting the place before it became their home was fun for Katie because of the laundry's bustling activity and sweet smell of scented soap. A glad day came in the summer when her mother's employer moved his laundry operations to a new location not far away, and Catherine had been able to get the room for a good price. Autumn had come now, and for all the mold and filth, it still smelled of fresh soap.

"I could leave school to help more."

"No, you're lucky to have the charity school. You'll need your education, and I don't mind the work."

Her mother's response pleased Katie. She loved school.

Catherine tied off the blue thread she was using and cut it with her crooked, yellow teeth.

"Should you take good care of yourself and your family," she said with a reflective sigh, "there shall always be something of beauty in your life, something sterling." She leaned toward Katie and cradled the girl's chin in her hand. The hand of a scourer, it felt rough, but Katie didn't mind. "I have *you*," Catherine said with a fragile smile. Her face held deep lines and a permanent look of worry, but it was the most warm and loving face there ever was.

When her mother said, "something sterling," she meant a thing *good and pure,* but because Katie liked the shine and high worth of silver, she always imagined it was the metal Catherine spoke about. Merely touching the silver of the thimble on her finger brought a thrill.

"Perhaps Christopher will bring something home for supper," Catherine said. Katie's brother and sisters, Christopher, Emma and Margaret, had gone to the West End to work as crossing-sweepers. When their earnings were good, they brought home fish.

Katie pushed the thought away to concentrate on sewing instead of hunger. Although it was foolish to think a silver thimble worked any better than a tin one, the silver definitely made pushing the needle and thread through cloth and buttons easier. She did a better job than before and with greater speed. Something about *silver* spoke of swiftness, but she couldn't remember what it was. If she had her own silver thimble, what couldn't she accomplish?

Catherine's work as a scourer was never enough. She took odd jobs where she found them and Katie helped any way she could. Katie knew her contribution to the welfare of the family was what kept her mother going. She'd rarely resented helping Catherine, but she did have ideas for improving their situation.

"If we took in mending work from Aunt Elizabeth—"

"You know I won't," Catherine said, her words bitten off short.

"Yes, but I don't understand why." Katie had spoken the words calmly, hoping her mother would soften her tone.

"I will have nothing from that man." Clearly Catherine struggled to maintain her composure.

"Uncle William?" Though usually in his cups, he seemed harmless.

"That's enough of that," Catherine said. "I cannot expect you to understand." The crackling tension in her voice turned into wet coughing and she bent forward. Her frequent hacking spells became worse on days like today when the dense, yellow fog, known as London Particular, hung over the city. Alarmed by the duration of the spell, Katie set aside her sewing and hugged her mother.

Finally Catherine sat back and wiped her mouth on a stained handkerchief.

"Feel better?" Katie asked.

Catherine waved away her concern. After a moment, she said, "I love my sister, but her husband is not a good man. We'll leave it at that."

"Yes, Mum. I don't mean to upset you."

Katie reached to take her mother's hand, then caught herself and tried to abort the gesture. Too late; the bright silver of the thimble on her finger had caught her mother's attention.

Katie expected her to be angry, but Catherine gently removed the thimble from her finger and returned it to the sewing kit. "You know you should use a more sensible one. The tin thimbles work just as well. If you must have something fancy, use the porcelain one."

"Why have it if you don't use it?" Katie's words came short and fast.

"It's a pretty thing and that's all," Catherine said, obviously trying to remain calm. "You were not to use the silver thimble and still you took it. Nothing good will come from such dishonesty. It is certainly not ladylike."

Katie balked at the idea. "If I were a lady, I'd have plenty of silver thimbles as well as other riches."

"At thirteen years, you're not a child anymore. Your temper

will only bring trouble. Others will judge you harshly for it. Take caution from the example of your cousin, Charles. He is too young to be drinking and fighting the way he does. He has spent more than one night in the drum. Life is not all cakes and ale. He'll come to no good."

Katie didn't like to hear that. Despite Charles's carousing and arrests, he was her favorite cousin. Three years older, he'd caught her eye and she his, but their mothers had kept them apart. Katie resented that.

She frowned, took a tin thimble from the sewing kit and turned her chair so that she faced away from Catherine before returning to her work.

"Life is hard on pretty girls, Katie. Pretty girls want things and have ways of getting them. Be careful what you do, to get what you want."

Katie liked to hear that she was pretty, yet didn't like the wistful tone in her mother's voice.

"Yes, still a girl, but then you're also a young woman," Catherine said.

Katie smiled, despite her foul mood, and was glad her mother couldn't see it.

"We are two poor women," Catherine said, "among many, gathered in the dim corners of London. Like the coal soot what falls everywhere—you don't mind it until it collects in your home, your kitchen, your bed. Then it's a nuisance that must be swept away into the street. Don't become a nuisance, Katie."

She says I'm a pretty woman, then spoils it calling me soot.

"One day," Catherine said, "the silver thimble shall be yours. You'll wear all the pretty off the outside using it. I know you will. I hope it takes many years. Take care you don't wear yourself out the way your poor mum has. But even so, should you do what you know to be right, like that thimble, there shall always be a bit of pretty on the inside. That's what keeps me going."

The pretty? The silver? Something good and pure? Does she mean inside herself, inside me, or the thimble?

Though difficult to understand at times, Mum meant well.

Katie knew that her mother sacrificed her health and happiness to provide for her children.

Catherine was so good, it was easy to imagine that pretty white metal lay just beneath her skin. But no, silver was hard and rigid, and her mother would be incapable of movement with all that inside her.

Then Katie remembered quicksilver. That was the something *swift* about silver. Her brother, Christopher, had once brought home a small bottle of the shiny liquid when he worked at a percussion cap factory.

Now, her mother was good and pure, filled with the pretty metal, and she could move again.

Katie imagined that bleeding a bit of quicksilver would be a sure sign of her own goodness. *To have that gift from Mum,* she told herself, *would be to always have her with me.*

Catherine's growling stomach interrupted Katie's thoughts, reminding her of the ache in her own belly and that she was supposed to be angry. She turned to her mother. "If you'll not use the thimble, then we should sell it."

"That isn't for you to decide. Were a gift from my sister."

Katie didn't really want it sold. She wanted to break her mother's rigid thinking about it. The thimble was a wonder that helped work go faster and made it more pleasurable. "Perhaps you're too proud to take good advice from a child."

"Such impertinence!" Catherine raised her hand to slap Katie across the mouth, but a shade of misery darkened her face and she flew into another coughing fit. Katie winced to see her cough bright blood into her handkerchief.

Life in the old laundry room was suddenly fragile. Gone were Katie's illusions that her efforts supported the family, that somehow the thimble would be the key to their success. A dread of the future welled up in her small frame, but she pushed it back down and held her mother. Finally Catherine leaned back and wiped her mouth and nose.

"I'm so sorry, Mum," Katie said. "I am such a wicked—"

"No, child, you are just hungry—hungry in many ways." She

reached into the sewing kit and pulled out the thimble and set it on the table beside her handkerchief. "It's for you."

Katie's eyes grew wide and she tried to look at it, but all she could see was the indelible red on the handkerchief.

The London Particular was so heavy the day Catherine died, gas lamps on the streets were lit at midday. Katie chose to believe they were lit for her mother.

She and her siblings were the only persons in attendance at Catherine's funeral. The stretch of marsh near St. Bride's Church that held her mother's grave gave off an odor like rotten eggs. The heavy fog, still present, created a wall around the burial party that was too close and contained too little air. Katie turned away in shame as Catherine's body was dumped, along with the corpses of three others, into a pauper's grave. The clergyman mumbled prayers and raggedy gravediggers shoveled clotted soil back into the deep, wet hole.

"We should save what money we can to have her taken from here and buried properly in hallowed ground," Katie said, her voice unsteady and cracking with emotion.

Christopher frowned, looked at his feet, shifted from foot to foot.

"The minister says we have six months," Emma said. "After that, they'll not open the grave."

"We have little now and in six months we may have less," Christopher said in a hurried way, sounding too practical for a sixteen-year-old. He still had the pink cheeks and thin blonde hair of a child. "You know how she likes people. She has company here. I'm sure they'll get along famously."

Perhaps he talked about their mother as if she were still alive to soften the blow of their loss. His way was to joke when things were hard.

"You could agree to try," Margaret said, holding tears back.

"Very well." Christopher nodded a little too vigorously to be believed, but they all let it go.

~ ~ ~

Katie and her older siblings were evicted from their dwelling. Christopher left for the industrial school to become a cobbler. Emma and Margaret found themselves in the workhouse. Katie went to live with her Aunt Elizabeth.

Choosing among her mother's possessions to carry away with her, Katie favored those items that held her mother's scent; a green alpaca skirt, a blue cotton skirt with a red flounce, bedclothes and a pillow.

A week after Catherine's death, on a chill, damp Tuesday night in the winter of 1855, Katie crossed the threshold and entered for the first time her Aunt Elizabeth's house in South Bermondsey. Although a much finer home than she'd ever hoped to live in, the quality of it made little impression. She moved in a daze, hugging the pillow, wearing the bedclothes like an outer garment and carrying everything else she owned, slung over her shoulder in her mother's old leather travel bag.

Her friend, her teacher, her confidant, her love was gone. Feeling abandoned and alone in the world, she was greeted by her aunt and uncle without ceremony.

"I'll not make sacrifices to see that she's fed," Uncle William said, eyeing her curiously.

"We'll manage somehow," Aunt Elizabeth said, leading Katie to a small room with shelves of textile supplies on either side of a small, makeshift bed. "You've said I needed help for some time."

"But a live-in?" William said with a scowl.

The aunt looked Katie in the eye. "You'll do your part, won't you?"

Katie could only nod her head.

"When I address you," Elizabeth said, her expression severe, "you will respond with words and use my name."

"Yes, Aunt Elizabeth," Katie said mechanically.

Her aunt's expression became severe. She took Katie's travel bag and placed it on the floor beside the door. "Now give me those filthy bedclothes and that wretched pillow."

Suddenly alert, Katie said, "No, please, Aunt Elizabeth. They are my Mum, my home."

"Catherine is gone, girl. This is your new home." Aunt Elizabeth snatched the items from her and hurried from the room.

Katie would have chased after her, but Uncle William stood

in the doorway staring. Confused and numb, Katie merely stood, looking at her feet and the rough floorboards. He lingered, his eyes moving up and down her length, then he left abruptly, shutting the door behind him.

Katie climbed in the bed, put her head on the unfamiliar pillow and pulled the covers up around her slight form. She had never been in such a warm, clean bed.

Why can't I feel it?

Strange and unwelcoming, she would trade it in an instant for another night in her own bed and one more goodnight kiss from Catherine. She tossed off the covers, fetched her mother's alpaca skirt from her travel bag and curled up with it on the floor, breathing in Catherine's scent.

Not my home. I may have to stay a while, but I'll find my own home one day and start a new life.

At some point in the night she awoke, cold and sore from the rough floorboards biting into her. Katie tossed the skirt into the bed and climbed up after it. She hid it under the pillow, pulled the covers up over herself and went back to sleep.

A Piece of White Coarse Linen

When Catherine's bedclothes and pillow were returned to Katie cleaned, her mother's scent was all but gone from them. She hid her mother's skirts by day so her aunt wouldn't clean them, and at night she retrieved and slept with them both.

Aunt Elizabeth, a seamstress, was a strict disciplinarian and taskmistress, clearly in charge of the household. Nothing was given to Katie that she didn't earn through hard work. She had little time for herself, yet was allowed to finish her final year of education at the Bermondsey United Charity School for Girls. For that, she felt grateful, even though Aunt Elizabeth required her to compensate for the time lost by working whatever hours were left to her after her lessons, mostly at night. Her duties included mending, alterations, stain removal, and garment dyeing, all services Aunt Elizabeth offered her customers.

Bent over a wash tub, Katie was cleaning a stained dress bodice the first time Uncle William lifted her skirts to touch her backside. She stood and turned quickly to defend herself, nearly upsetting the tub. Uncle William, a crooked smile on his leering face, backed away swiftly and left the room. Too embarrassed to say anything about it, Katie kept her shock and dismay to herself.

That is what Mum wouldn't tell me about him.

Over time, his pawing became a habit. He took advantage of the times when she was absorbed in her work to grab at her budding breasts or reach under her skirts. She endured the indignity with as much grace as possible and became ever watchful while working alone. Sticking close to Aunt Elizabeth during waking hours, though not the most pleasant way to spend her days, prevented the worst of his abuses.

~ ~ ~

Katie had been with her aunt and uncle for a year when, through the front windows of the house, she saw gaunt figures approaching along the lane in the hazy-bright, midday sun. Recognizing her sisters, she ran out the front door to hug them, but stopped short when close, overcome by their smell. Thin and dirty, they had aged ten years in the span of only one. Clearly they were her sisters—their features were nearly the same and they still had the dark, almost black hair of their mother. They wore the same clothes they'd worn a year earlier, Emma in a worn brown linsey-woolsey skirt and bodice, Margaret in gray and blue wool. Even so, Katie found a frightful madness in their appearance, as if she were facing dangerous, savage strangers, for who would willingly allow themselves to fall into such a state? They were mottled with sores and abrasions, and a weary animal vigilance haunted their eyes. Katie wanted to reject the reality of what she saw. Indeed, she looked for evidence that her sisters were actors wearing costumes.

The three stood for a moment regarding each other silently, then Katie overcame her fear and hurried to hug them. With each embrace, she worried she might catch lice and disease.

"It's good to see you," Katie said, though she wasn't at all certain she felt the truth of it. She offered her sisters a grim smile and furrowed brow.

"Thank you," Emma said. "I'm sorry we didn't come sooner. A leave of absence is a misery of documents and we must give up our uniforms and don our old clothes."

"Come say hello to your aunt and uncle."

Aunt Elizabeth stood in the front doorway, arms crossed, barring passage. "We're expecting a customer," she said.

Katie, who commonly knew the day's schedule, was unaware of that.

"You two are too filthy to come in," Elizabeth continued. "If you'll go to the rear, I'll bring you something to eat."

Emma and Margaret made no response to the rudeness.

Katie led them to the back of the house. "I'm sorry," she said when they were out of earshot of their aunt. They sat in the sun, amidst barrels and crates at the back doorstep. Elizabeth provided them with a midday meal of boiled cabbage, potatoes and bacon. Katie pretended she was not hungry and offered up her portion to her sisters. They ate what lay on their plates with a slow determination, then scrupulously divided and ate what was on hers.

Margaret had temporarily lost her voice due to a case of influenza. She communicated with smiles and nods. Sneezing repeatedly, she blew her nose into a piece of coarse linen.

Emma showed reluctance to talk about the workhouse as Katie plied her with questions. "We are clothed and kept warm," Emma said, finally opening up, "but are rarely fed more than a thin gruel. The staff is corrupt and abusive and must be paid in some way for any advantage. We share beds with strangers, several over a month's time. That means sharing their illnesses. The work is hard and the hours long. Look at my hands." She held up cracked and scabbed fingers. "Courtesy of the Lump Hotel. Most of the work is picking oakum for the ship builders."

Regretting her persistence, Katie frowned and turned away, looking for a way to change the subject. "Have you heard anything from Christopher?"

"No, we haven't." Emma said sadly. "I don't know if he is earning his keep yet, but he were right about us." Her words came out thick and slurred.

"What do you mean?" Katie asked.

"That we would not earn enough to have Mother placed in hallowed ground. It's too late now. I hope she enjoys her companions." Emma chuckled dryly and Margaret bowed her head and closed her eyes as if nodding off.

Katie thought Emma was being disrespectful, but then had a brief, pleasing image of Catherine playing Grandmother's Trunk with her grave companions. The game was Katie's favorite to play with her mother while they replaced buttons in the evening.

A pleasant way for her to while away eternity.

"I met a man, Joseph Matthews, in the workhouse," Emma said slowly, a faraway look in her eyes. "He found work as a lumper and has left us...for a time. We're to be married...soon as he's earned enough to find suitable lodgings. I'll take Margaret with me."

Margaret glanced up briefly with a flicker of a smile, but otherwise remained motionless.

"I'm pleased to hear of the hope Mr. Matthews brings," Katie said.

The food seemed to have put her sisters in a stupor. They didn't offer anything more to the immediate conversation.

Katie tried unsuccessfully to think of something else to say. She had become uncomfortable and wanted their visit to end, and was ashamed of that desire. Still, she was in sympathy with her aunt; as long as her sisters were living in the workhouse—Emma had called it the Lump Hotel—Katie wanted nothing to do with them either.

She flinched and drew her hand back when she felt Margaret's touch. Her silent sister had reached for her *so* quietly.

"She wants to hold your hand," Emma said.

Katie had the absurd fear that the workhouse might rub off on her.

Margaret's eyes expressed hurt.

"You startled me is all," Katie said, and grasped her sister's rough, scabby fingers in her own.

She felt a great relief when they left to return to the workhouse in the late afternoon. Her sisters were mere ghosts of the young women they had been, particularly the silent Margaret.

Katie fell into a state of mourning while cleaning up after their meal. Finding the piece of linen Margaret had used as a handkerchief, she could not throw it away. She washed it and added it to her possessions.

A White Handle Table Knife, a Ticking Pocket, and a Cork

With time Katie became resigned to William reaching under her skirts because she always managed to keep her drawers on. Then, when she was sixteen years old, he became more insistent. To insure her safety, she took a sharp table knife from the kitchen and made a pocket to hide it in. She made the pocket from a section of the blue striped bed ticking from her mother's pillow with strings added to cinch the opening around the handle of the knife. Adding a band to the pocket allowed her to fastened it around her waist out of sight, under her top skirt. A cork stuck on the end of the knife prevented it from cutting through the bottom of the pocket. Although difficult to get to in a hurry, she felt better having some form of protection.

One day, nearly sober, Uncle William came to her while she stood at a work table preparing a cochineal dye bath for a customer's faded red jacket. He reached for her. Katie dodged and upset the bath, spilling bright crimson dye over several bolts of cloth.

"Your aunt shall be unhappy you've wasted her dyestuffs and damaged her valuable goods," Uncle William said. "I might agree with her that you should be turn out of our home. However, should you be good to me, I shall tell her *I* upset the dye bath."

Cast out on the street with no where to go but the workhouse, the grueling life under conditions of hard labor, malnourishment and chronic disease—that was all too much to face.

Katie allowed Uncle William to have his way. In his excitement, he ejaculated too soon, merely staining her drawers.

She pushed her skirts back down and started cleaning up the spilled dye. Uncle William was straightening his clothing when Aunt Elizabeth came in. She looked at him, her brow furrowed and mouth open with an unspoken question. Then she saw the spilled dye on the table and her eyes turned on Katie.

"What have you done, girl?" She grabbed Katie by the arm and pulled her roughly away from her work and turned her around. "Do you know what this dye and cloth cost me?" Aunt Elizabeth backhanded her across the mouth, splitting her lip. Katie cringed silently.

"Answer me, child!"

"*I* spilled the bath," Uncle William said.

Aunt Elizabeth spun on him.

"You asked me to wax the sash." He pointed to the window behind the table, his head tilted to one side and his mouth pinched with false remorse. "I should have waited for her to move her work. I'm sorry, love."

"Where is the wax?" she demanded to know.

He shrugged. "I were trying the window first."

She looked at him hard, the suspicion on her face unwavering. Then she turned back to Katie. "Clean this up at once."

"Yes, Aunt Elizabeth," Katie said, as her aunt swept from the room. Relief was overshadowed by a deep dread of the future with Uncle William.

"Good girl," he said, and left her to her work.

To get by, I'll always be beholden to someone. I must find one who will not charge a cruel price.

~ ~ ~

Uncle William came to her often after that, but drunk most of the time, he wasn't interested in surveying his conquest and his aim was poor. If she squeezed her legs tightly together, he responded as if he had achieved penetration. These hot, sweaty transactions were disgusting, but his release, attended by much huffing and puffing of his sour swill breath, always came quickly.

A Man's White Waistcoat

At the age of nineteen, Katie felt a bit foolish that she still slept with her mother's skirts. Even so, she cuddled with them at night, pressing the fabric against her nose, trying to retrieve the long-gone scent of her dear Catherine. The only time she felt close to her mother was when she held the thimble.

Most of the silver had worn off the outside, and Katie thought the *pretty* had all but worn off her as well. Still, each time she put her finger in the thimble, she remembered what her mother had said about the silver inside, and she liked to think there remained something *good and pure* in her as well. Whenever she bled she hoped to see a bit of quicksilver mingled with her blood. Although a childish fantasy, looking for it became something of a game that was harmless and yet helped distract from the fright of bleeding.

She was touching the silver inside the thimble when she met Conway. The year was 1861. He was close to thirty years old, tall and fair. A round-topped felt hat and side whiskers framed his friendly face. His brown, striped trousers were worn shiny at the thighs, thin at the knees. He came to her needing the green revers of his white, square-cut linsey waistcoat mended.

Aunt Elizabeth was known to accept work through her kitchen window in the early evening. Katie was working alone in the kitchen at the time, her aunt having been called away to attend to an ailing neighbor. She was singing a favorite ballad of her mother's when he approached.

"My name is Tom," he said. "People call me Conway."

His waistcoat was ratty, but he offered it through the open window as if it were precious.

"It is the uniform of a poet, Miss," he said, his accent making it obvious he was Irish. "It has seen many a glorious campaign, but is become old and gloomy. Please revive its spirits, for I must look my best. I'll wait, if you don't mind."

"Not at all," she said.

His whiskers had worn away the green cloth at the sides of the garment's neck—a common problem. "I don't have cloth to fill what's missing, but I can darn it with a matching thread."

"I trust you will do your best."

Conway remained throughout the mending, leaning on the sill, gazing off down the lane, trying to look relaxed and care free. He obviously posed for her. Under the guise of keeping himself amused, he whistled a tune and recited a couple of sonnets Katie knew to be by William Shakespeare.

"I heard you singing 'The Berkshire Tragedy,'" he said. "If you like sad songs, you might like this one." He sang a popular gallows ballad.

"Of a dreadful Murder you shall soon hear,
Was done in Banbury, in Oxfordshire;
One William Willson, how sad to tell;
Murdered Susan Owen, who was known full well.
The murderer Willson, so cruel he,
Slew Sarah Owen, aged thirty-three."

Conway was quite handsome and clever. He was indeed trying to impress her, but there was something different in the way he went about it. The majority of men who chased after her were either drunk or acted as if they were. If she'd thought any had prospects for the future she might well have chased after them to escape her situation with Uncle William and her cold-hearted aunt.

Conway, while whimsical, had a sense of purpose about him. He was sober and respectful. When he stole glances at her during his performance, her heart skipped a beat or two because he did it in a discreet manner refreshingly different from the ogling she usually got.

"In a dreary dungeon he now bewails,
Awaiting his trial in Oxford Jail,
And if he should there convicted be,
His days must end on the fatal tree…"

He paused when he was done, no doubt for dramatic effect, looking pensively thoughtful. Then he turned to Katie and said, "I penned that sad tale."

Although he was probably lying about writing the ballad, his attention and efforts to impress were flattering. *The silver has not worn off the outside of me entirely. Perhaps he'll take me away from here and give me a new life, a new home.*

Foolishness! But what harm in fantasy if you know it's just that.

"Did you enjoy it?" Conway asked.

Katie merely looked up from her work, smiled and nodded.

Conway fixed his gaze on her, and, after a moment, said, "You're a pretty girl. I have use for a pretty girl. How are you at hawking?"

Speechless and flustered, Katie made an effort to relax and smile, to regain her voice and allow her blushing face to loose its telltale color. Perhaps he would think she was merely choosing words carefully.

"I'm quite good at it," she said, finally. "As a child, I sold watercress at Farringdon Market."

"Good," he said. "Would you care to accompany me to a hanging?"

As Katie considered his curious invitation, the musical sound of jars and bottles bumping into one another came from behind her. Since Uncle William was insensible in his bedroom, she presumed Aunt Elizabeth had returned and was moving around in the spence off the adjoining hall.

Katie's answer was quick and whispered, "Yes."

Conway glanced deeper into the house, then his eyes returned to Katie. "I'll collect you at dawn," he said quietly.

~ ~ ~

Katie awakened in the night. Excited about the coming day, she struggled in and out of sleep for the next few hours. When a thin slice of sunlight cut across her small storeroom window, she got up and prepared for the day, then moved to the front of the house to watch for Conway through a window.

He appeared in the lane and she opened the door.

"You'll not be going with that Irishman," came her aunt's voice from behind.

Heart in throat, Katie turned around.

Aunt Elizabeth, cinching her gown, moved to close the front door as Conway reached the doorstep. Before it swung shut in his face, he stumbled back.

Aunt Elizabeth struck at Katie, trying to box her ear. Katie retreated, holding her hands out to fend off the attack.

"You would bring shame on us," Aunt Elizabeth spat, "after all we've done for you?"

"I've done nothing to cause shame," Katie said, "and I work for my bed and board. Every day!"

She reversed course and moved toward Aunt Elizabeth, and was rewarded when the woman backed away, eyes wide. Her aunt clearly struggled to say something or keep from saying something. Katie had always thought of her as formidable, but in conflict, they were well-matched. She grabbed a chair from beside the door and placed it between them.

Aunt Elizabeth bared her stained teeth. "Without us you'd be with your sisters in the Lump Hotel. That's where I ought to send you."

"Don't threaten me." Anger burned in Katie's belly and her eyes flashed with the fire in her heart.

"You work for me. You owe us everything."

"This man has offered me work, and I would bring my earnings to you."

"I shan't accept such ill-gotten gains," Aunt Elizabeth cried, stamping her foot as if Katie's neck were beneath it. "It's bad enough you've seduced your uncle."

Katie froze.

Her aunt had a grim smile. "Oh yes, I know what you two have been up to."

Katie's anger eclipsed the shame of being exposed. "Yes, Aunt Elizabeth, Uncle William also thinks I owe everything." Her teeth bore down on one another until they hurt, but it kept her from lashing out physically. "Soon I shall have nothing left."

She turned and retreated into her storeroom. She listened at her door for a time and, after a moment, Aunt Elizabeth could be heard returning to her bedroom. Katie quietly opened the window and climbed through. Out of breath, she caught up with Conway at the end of the lane.

"You must go back," he said, a look of concern darkening his face. "You don't want to sacrifice everything for a little adventure."

Katie shrugged. "Aunt Elizabeth has debt and takes on too much work." She spoke with a dismissive tone and a defiant, lopsided hitch to her lower lip. "Uncle William is worse than useless. He drinks up her earnings. She cannot get along without me."

"Well, then," Conway said, smiling, "I'm glad you'll come along."

~ ~ ~

They traveled in an omnibus to Newgate Prison for the hanging. The vehicle was so crowded Conway placed Katie in his lap. A woman sitting across from them glared disapprovingly.

She's dressed to the nines, while the man next to her is square rigged. He's with her, but they should be more at home in a carriage. Perhaps

they have been reduced and the clothes and her manner are the last of
her finery. Katie gave the woman a warm, sympathetic smile.

As she and Conway were beginning to get stares from others,
he stated loudly that she was his new bride. As proof, he held up
his left hand to display a brass ring on his ring finger that she had
not noticed before. Katie blushed. Laughter and good cheer filled
the coach.

While the square rigged gentleman smiled, the elegantly-dressed
woman turned her face away and buried her nose in a sachet. Her
suddenly pale skin, pinched lips, and rolling eyes suggested she
might faint from the foul order of unwashed bodies surrounding
her.

*She must not be a Londoner. Everything has smelled so fresh and
new since the end of The Great Stink.*

Conversations among the passengers became louder and less
private until nearly all within the large coach seemed comfortable
responding and contributing to anything said. The talk revealed
that many were on their way to the hanging. As news and witticism
were shared, it was as if the passengers were together as one on
a great adventure. A jolly fat man named Ellis bragged that he'd
managed a great feat in getting himself, his wife, and eight children,
all of whom he introduced one at a time, on the same omnibus.
He told a humorous tale of a previous hanging they had attended
and of the dreadful fate of the condemned at the hands of *body-
snatchers* and *medical gentlemen.*

His stories made it more difficult to imagine where they were
going and what it would be like. Conway had asked Katie to help
him sell chapbooks to the crowd attending the hanging of Michael
Buseman. The chapbook consisted of several broadsheets folded
together, containing information about the man's life, crime, and
trial and a gallows ballad Conway had written meant to be sung
to the popular tune, "The Siren's Harp," by Arnold Scott. The
chapbooks were to be sold for a penny apiece.

"If we work hard," he'd said, "we might sell a thousand copies.
You'll earn a twentieth of the proceeds."

Katie had done the maths for herself. *That's four shillings and more!*

An erection grew in Conway's trousers as the coach bumped along. *If he'll share that with me, what more will he share? He paid for us to ride the omnibus! He's a generous soul with income more than sufficient for his needs. Perhaps I shall have a new life.*

When the vehicle bounced over uneven road, she allowed it to cover a little extra movement of her own against Conway's lap. Clearly aware of what she was doing, he planted a moist kiss on her lips. Katie smiled. Her heart raced and she struggled to catch her breath as the coach erupted in cheers.

An image of Aunt Elizabeth's angry face came unbidden. *She will be so angry with me, but I don't care. I've taken little time for myself.*

~ ~ ~

Throngs of people filled the street where they departed the omnibus near Newgate Prison. Never had there been so much confused noise.

Conway paused to tie a beautiful red gauze silk kerchief around Katie's neck. "There you are," he said. "A fine billy to enhance your beauty and make you easier to find in the crowd should you become lost."

"A gift?" she asked. "It's too much."

No, he might take it back!

"I intend you shall work it off." He said with a warm smile.

"Is it a romantic gesture," Katie asked, with beguiling eyes, "part of a business deal, or merely useful?"

"Could it not be all three?" Conway asked.

He is clever indeed. "Yes, I suppose it could."

Conway touched her cheek tenderly before turning back to business. "We'll make our way along Newgate Street to Old Bailey." He pointed toward the corner of the ugly stone prison building. "That's where my printer shall meet us with my chap books."

The people were a river of conflicting currents filling the street. Some time would pass before Katie and Conway arrived at their destination, but he seemed in no hurry.

"Is everyone in the world here today?" she asked, her eyes wide.

"No, lass," he said with a straight face. "So many didn't know you were coming."

She grinned, and he did as well, with a slight bow to his head and a twinkle in his eye.

While Conway removed his knee-length, brown top coat and began turning it inside out, Katie surveyed the crowd. Few gentlemen and ladies occupied the street. Most of the throng were laborers, with a few vendors mixed in. Children were everywhere, shouting at the top of their lungs and moving swiftly between the adults. Every way she turned, Katie found eyes. While some expressed a festive mood, other eyes held anger, mistrust, lust or even hatred. The whole was a pandemonium of sound, color and movement. Dizzy, Katie closed her eyes momentarily, but Conway caught her by the arm as he began to move.

"Keep your wits about you," he said. "The crowd is full of pickpockets, ruffians, and thieves who cause no end of mischief. Don't worry about what you're stepping on. Keep your eyes up and looking around. Don't let the children get too close. They'll rob you blind and you'll not know it till it's too late."

Katie followed, doing as she was told.

I have nothing of value but the silk neckerchief. Should they take it without me knowing, they can have it."

When we arrive at Old Bailey, you'll see the portable gallows. They erect it in front of the Debtors' Door. We'll not get too close to it because that's where the crowd does its worst violence. We're not here to see the man dangle. We're here to sell poetry!"

The printer, a thin, ink-stained man, who smelled of bad fish and had no teeth, stood at the corner of Newgate and Old Bailey as promised. He passed Conway several bundles of chapbooks tied with yellow string. Once paid, the man disappeared into the crowd. Conway cut the string on one bundle and handed it to Katie.

"You're to shout 'A Sorrowful Lamentation of Michael Buseman, just one penny,'" Conway explained. "If we remain at this corner, the crowd will move around us. We'll stand back to back. You'll face south. I'll face east. Keep the extra bundles beneath you, under your skirts. Should someone give you trouble, I'll be right here.

slit." He indicated an intentionally split but finished seam in the side of his long brown top coat. "Do you understand?"

"Yes," she said. Again, her heart raced. Butterflies fluttered in her stomach and a thrill ran along her spine. Was it fear or pleasure? She couldn't decide. *It's always like this with Conway.*

Katie had hardly spoken her sales pitch when a young man offered a shiny, new penny. As sales of the chapbook became routine during the next couple of hours, she became calm again. Too calm, perhaps, as her lack of vigilance may have shown in her eyes.

A man in a long, blue coat and black bowler hat stepped up, made as if to draw a coin from his pocket, and instead came up with a knife. Brandishing his weapon, he gave her a hard look, then grabbed for the bundle of chapbooks in her left hand.

Katie was not going to let him take them. She held on and cried out, but feared she could not be heard in the surrounding maelstrom of noise.

The man swung with the knife. Katie dropped down onto the bundles beneath her skirt and leaned away to the right and raised her left arm inside the arc of the weapon. Her wrist took a slice against the bone as the thief pulled back for another strike. Katie drew her arm away, rolled off the bundle onto the pavement, her hip grinding painfully against the table knife in its pocket under her skirt. She could use it for defense, but she wouldn't be able get to it in time. She rolled again, then looked up to see Conway take a swing at the man. The expression of surprise on the thief's face burst into one of pain as Conway's fist struck him in the eye. the stranger staggered back, rebounding off a young couple holding hands and nearly knocking them down. The bowler hat fell from his head and he dashed off into the crowd.

Conway helped her to her feet. Katie held up her bundle of chapbooks.

"Good Girl. You defend my merchandise—" He stooped to pick up the bowler, which was old and worn, but much finer than his own hat. "—and win me a bowler too. Aren't you a find?" He gave out a large and powerful laugh and his eyes became those of

a kind father.

Katie blinked away rising tears of relief. Pride swelled in her chest as he looked upon her with such tenderness.

Conway saw the wound on her arm and his features became pinched with concern. "You're hurt."

Heart beat pounding in her neck, Katie's ears buzzed and her vision, painting everything with unusually vivid colors and crisps edges, shivered with each pulse. Again, looking for quicksilver in her blood, she watched the rapid drip from her wrist while Conway took a white handkerchief from his coat. *Should the silver liquid flow now, he shall think I am very special indeed.*

What a silly thought! I must be out of my mind from the fear.

He wrapped the handkerchief about her wrist to stanch the flow of blood. "There now," he said. "You'll be as good as new."

"I'm well enough," she said. "Let's continue with our sales." Truly, she didn't want to turn away from him and lose sight of those warm eyes, but that was what he'd want.

Midway through the afternoon of selling, a bell began to toll. A cry of "Hat's off" went up and passed around the crowd. Some of the people became still and stood clutching their hats with their heads bowed. A commotion at the gallows drew most everyone's attention for a time and then a great cheer rose up from the horde. After that the crowd slowly began to disperse.

Conway's coat had become heavy. Katie was exhausted, and her shoes were filthy with horse dung and other substances she could not identify. They had sold eight-hundred and seventy-nine copies of the chapbook. Conway looked pleased.

"If you are willing," he said, "I'd like your help with sales again soon."

"I would help now if I could," Katie said.

"No, you must go home. I'll collect you in a week for an execution in Southwark."

She did not look forward to the inevitable confrontation with Aunt Elizabeth. "But I don't have to return right away."

"Yes, you do. I cannot take you with me. We must protect your reputation against the unkindness of the world."

His concern was thoughtful, but Katie wasn't happy about it. She became quiet as he escorted her back to her aunt's home in the early evening, first riding the omnibus and then walking. Perhaps her five percent earning of the day's sales would be sufficient to soften Elizabeth's heart.

When they arrived, she discovered her old travel bag, stuffed to overflowing, sitting beside the back doorstep.

It might have been taken! Katie plunged her hand into it and felt around. She took a deep breath and relaxed when her fingers located her thimble. The bag held all her possessions except for her mother's pillow.

Katie tried the door, found it locked.

I have no home! Images of the workhouse, conjured by Emma's descriptions, filled her head.

She pounded on the door. With no response, she ran to the front of the house. The door was locked. She knocked, and when no answer came, she rattled it mercilessly.

Katie was trying to look through the curtained windows as Conway caught up with her. He stood, tall and proud, holding her travel bag.

"Come with me," he said.

He will protect me. I must make sure to please him.

Katie flew to Conway. He wrapped his arms about her and led her away.

Conway rented a single room in a tenement in Westminster with its own street level entrance. Having stopped at a tavern for a meal of potato pie and stewed mutton and ox cheek, they arrived late in the night. The richness of the meal and her fatigue left Katie warmly intoxicated. She fought against her languor. Her heart told her she could trust Conway, but with no home to return to, and having to depend on his good graces, Katie knew she was vulnerable.

Conway located his key and glanced up and down the street, seemingly concerned about their safety or, perhaps, merely being seen. Satisfied that all was well, he fitted the key into the padlock on the door and opened it. He ushered her inside and quickly shut the door behind them.

When total darkness pressed in on Katie, her torpor fled and she became fully alert.

My life is all darkness now. I can't see the future, how to live and earn a crust. What shall Conway expect of me?

No answers came from within. The combined blindness fed a rising panic.

As Conway fumbled about in the dark, perhaps locating a weapon with which to end her life, alarm rose in Katie, making its way to her throat. She would scream and then surely he would *have* to kill her.

A match struck, a candle lit, and the scream died in her throat. She stepped back from her fear and there, before her, lay an avenue into the future. The room was neat as a pin, bed made, table in one corner with items, mostly paper, stacked evenly, shelving bearing folded clothing and organized chapbooks. The air smelled heavily of Conway, and an odor of aged slops, perhaps from an overflowing cesspit in the cellar, a common problem in these old tenements. A Soyer stove, its pipe routed through a makeshift hole in the wall, shared one corner with a tub for bathing. The room felt a bit like a cell, having no windows. Still, it was well-organized and not unwelcoming.

Katie had little choice but to trust Conway, but it didn't *feel* wrong to do so.

"Please sit," Conway said, gesturing toward his bed. He took a seat at the table, lit a lamp and concentrated on counting his money. Katie stood for a moment awkwardly, unwilling at first to sit on a man's bed. Since there was nowhere else, she finally sat on the edge and watched Conway.

She expected he would count out her earnings and offer them to her, but that didn't happen. When finished counting, he scooped all the pennies into a blue and white crockery jar, placed a lid on it and hid it on a low shelf behind a stack of chapbooks.

I'll ask him about it tomorrow.

Katie hastened to cover her yawning mouth as he turned to her with a smile. "If you have no nightdress," he said, "I have one that belonged to my sister you can wear."

He lifted a white cotton chemise from a shelf holding other clothing items. The fabric was so much thicker and nicer than the one Katie had in her travel bag, she reached for it without hesitation, then blushed.

He'll want to watch me put it on.

"Go ahead." Conway said, turning away. "I shan't look."

Katie quickly disrobed. She would keep the pillow ticking bag holding the table knife secured around her waist.

No, Conway might discover it.

She untied its bands and bundled it with her clothing and pushed it against the wall beside the bed, then pulled the chemise on over her head.

"The bed is large enough for us both," he said. "You mustn't worry about the safety of your virtue."

"Is that true?" Katie hoped her voice was steady. Whether or not she would give herself to him was dependent on how much she trusted Conway and what, if anything, was their future together. Again, her head and heart could not come to terms on how to proceed.

"You're a pretty girl whose attentions I crave, but I have no desire for a woman who doesn't want me."

He doesn't just take what he wants.

Katie climbed in the bed and moved to the side against the wall, pulled the covers up around her and lay back on a thin feather pillow. She should be on the side with the escape route, but how to say that to Conway?

"There may come a time when you might honor me in that way, but not tonight. We are both too tired." He extinguished the lamp and the candle.

She heard fumbling that sounded like undressing. Despite his words, he might climb in bed naked and press himself against her.

Perhaps I'd like that.

Even so, she drew back against the wall as he lifted the covers to climb in and draft of cool air hit her.

The warmth returned to the bed and he maintained a respectful distance.

I cannot tell if he's naked.

Both emotional letdown and a sense of relief took fear away. She folded the thin pillow and snuggled into it, breathing in Conway's strong scent.

In her exhaustion, she had a guarded thought, *I could do much worse than to marry a poet.*

She suppressed a giggle.

How foolish that I'd thought he might kill me!

As head and heart began to find common ground, Katie became giddy. She could reach for Conway, pull him to her and allow him to take her.

But she might not be ready.

Still, her heart insisted on some expression of her desire. She reached tentatively with a foot to touch him.

A thrill ran through her when he responded, his feet embracing her own.

Katie lay awake wondering what it all might mean until exhaustion claimed her.

A Ball of Hemp, Tin for Sugar, Tin for Tea, Flannel with Soap, Flannel with Sewing Needs

The next day, Katie failed to ask Conway about her one-twentieth of chapbook sales. She didn't ask about it the day after that either. Then, as the days turned into weeks and Conway provided everything in her new life, she decided she didn't need payment.

Despite the dampness of the district, Conway's room remained dry and cozy. Most of the time the smell from the cellar went unnoticed. Even when evident, the odor paled in comparison to the Great Stink of two years ealier, when the amount of waste entering the Thames and an unusually hot summer combined to create a miasma so potent it nearly shut down the government and brought the city to a halt. Those who could afford to do so evacuated the city. If she could survive that, there wasn't much else to fear in the realm of odor.

What little cooking Conway did—boiling vegetables and an occasional bit of meat, or heating water for tea and coffee—was done on the Soyer stove, also used to keep the room warm. But most of their meals were taken at the Adam and Eve Tavern a few streets to the West.

Conway's straw bed was lumpy and sweat-stained. Katie cleaned the ticking and bedclothes and did her best to redistribute the straw. He was grateful.

She sang songs in the mornings, starting with popular folk tunes, then learned to sing several of the gallows ballads Conway had written.

"Your beautiful voice gives life to my lyrics," Conway said.

"You must think I'm gulpy!" Katie said.

"No, truly, you have a beautiful voice. If I were a different man, I'd have you singing in all the pubs to promote our ballads."

So there it is. Always some angle to what he says and does. Still, he's good to me. And perhaps I do have a good voice.

With time, Katie came to like Conway's idea even if he didn't. One of the Adam and Eve's barmaids, Eloise Millican, told her that the landlord of the establishment had opened a back room for those willing to pay a little extra for some entertainment. "He listens to the sing-alongs among the customers," Eloise said. "Should he find a woman of the right talent, one who can present herself properly, he hires her to sing in his back room. The room doesn't have a name yet, but folks are calling it The Garden of Eden. I've heard that impresarios from some of the music halls are already coming to performances at The Garden, looking for talent."

"Is the landlord Mr. Senters, the gentleman with the red beard?" Katie asked.

"Yes, but he doesn't like folks to know he's listening. He wouldn't want me talking about it."

"No one shall know we spoke."

In talking about hopes for his ballads to become popular, Conway had explained that the quality of entertainment didn't vary much between the aristocratic music halls of Leicester Square and those of less fashionable parts of town or even the poor and squalid districts.

The clothes were the key, Katie had decided, for appearances accounted for much in life. She imagined herself fashionably dressed on stage in one of the great music halls in the West End, singing one of Conway's sad ballads, her exquisite performance bringing the audience to tears. With Conway's income, acquiring such finery was within the realm of possibility. Then she might catch the eye and the ear of the Adam and Eve's landlord, Mr. Senters.

Little time passed before Katie drew Conway into an embrace that led to sex. Unlike Uncle William, Conway *was* interested in how she looked under her skirts. She tried the trick she'd used on William, but Conway was not to be fooled. Penetration was indeed achieved, and Katie liked it.

She quickly came to see herself as invaluable to Conway. He worked hard to provide for them, and did well. Katie worked equally hard alongside him. She could never be an equal partner, but she wanted his respect and for her feelings and opinions to be a matter of consequence to him.

One afternoon as they were ducking out to get a bite to eat, Katie became annoyed with Conway furtively glancing up and down the street before they exited his room. "Must you sneak me in and out of your room day and night?" she asked.

"The neighbors will talk." He had a dismissive tone. "I'm protecting you from scorn."

"The neighbors have seen me," Katie said flatly. "They work too hard to care what you do."

Conway opened his mouth, clearly about to argue his point, then apparently thought better of it. "If the landlord hears about you, he'll raise my rent." He paused for a moment, then said, "I'll have a talk with him."

His decision to be honest was a good one. He was a different sort of man.

A teetotaler, Conway saved earnings he might have spent on drink. He had a pension from his years in the Eighteenth Irish Regiment, but his main source of income was his chapbooks.

Conway had a confederate at the Sessions House, the Criminal Court in the Old Bailey, and the new Court adjoining it, who brought him the latest news of cases that might end in a sentence of death. He had friends who sent him news from the legal courts in other cities. Conway worked on ballads for those he believed would be convicted. His goal was to have a ballad completed by the time the sentence was handed down. Rarely did one of his ballads go unpublished.

They traveled to Warwick, Worcester, and Stafford to sell chapbooks at public hangings. Katie prepared several necessities for their trips, a flannel and soap, another with pins and needles, a ball of hemp, a tin box with tea and another with sugar, and loaded them into her travel bag along with extra clothing for Conway and herself.

In the past, Conway had hired young men to travel with him and help with sales, but presently Katie was all he needed. To draw more attention to their product, he encouraged Katie to sing the ballads they were trying to sell. She had a good ear and a pure voice that she could project with great clarity over the din of the crowd.

She was delighted by the admiring looks she got and frequently imagined herself to be singing from a stage.

Most often Conway wrote his ballads at the Adam and Eve Tavern after he and Katie had eaten their evening meal. Sitting and smoking his pipe, obsessively sharpening the point on his pencil with a table knife, as if that might sharpen the effect of his words, Conway would grumble and scribble a line or two, then read it to Katie. She tired of it one evening and set aside the newspaper she was reading.

Looking around the tavern, she found Mr. Senters sitting alone at a table with a pint. Perhaps he was listening to the sing-alongs, looking for talent.

"If I had better clothing," Katie told Conway, "something more like a music hall singer might wear, I'd attract more of the crowd when I sing."

"I should say so," he said. "But a constable would come 'round and haul you off for indecency." He chuckled then. "I've been to music halls and seen the female singers. They can't sing two songs without a change of clothing. I can't afford that."

"Something with silk and velvet and a bit of color," she said. "Perhaps green. With that I might well find myself singing in a music hall one day."

"Don't get ahead of yourself," he said. "We're doing quite well as it is."

A group of young men and women at a nearby table, sang popular songs drunkenly. With her ability to project her voice, Katie knew she could fill the tavern with song and draw everyone's attention.

If Conway watches me capture the hearts of these people, he shan't be able to deny my need for fine clothes. And, should Mr. Senters be pleased with my voice, I might go on to sing in his back room.

"I'm going to ask those people if I might sing with them." she said.

But as Katie made to get up, Conway grabbed her roughly by the arm. "You'll not be associating with those who drink." The look in his eye grew severe and frightening.

"I'll sing here, then."

"You'll not make a scene," he demanded. He squeezed her arm uncomfortably, then let it go.

Katie, her plan thwarted, became ill-tempered, but didn't want to admit what she was up to. Still, she was not going to take Conway's abuse. She plucked the pipe from his mouth and stuck it in her own, she slouched in her seat to match his posture, she grumbled and pretended to scribble lines of poetry, all to mock him.

Conway chuckled at her antics, and she found it disarming. The spell cast by his anger was temporarily broken.

"Sitting with you while you write is tedious." Katie said. "If you want me to stay here, you'll speak to me."

Anger flashed briefly in his eyes, and then he relaxed. "I suppose there are times when I may be sitting next to you, but I'm not here. When I'm writing, my mind wanders off."

Katie watched Mr. Senters finish off his pint and slip behind the bar to continue his work.

Conway was in no mood to consider her needs.

Her plans would have to wait.

A Short Black Clay Pipe and a Tin Match Box

Sitting with Conway in the tavern when he wrote, Katie took to stealing his pipe for a few quick puffs whenever she became bored with whatever she'd brought to read. He didn't take it kindly, but she did get his attention that way. Once she had it, she'd at least manage to get a chuckle out of him. Soon that wasn't enough diversion and she decided to become more involved in what he was writing. She learned what she could about the subjects of the ballads, and when Conway became stuck, she'd invent a line or two of her own and offer them to him. Although Conway included her lines in his ballads, he never acknowledged her contributions until the day he gave her the gift of a short black clay pipe.

They were sitting at a corner table by a window at the Adam and Eve waiting for their dinner. Rain washed soot down the outside of the glass in delicate rivulets. Conway got Katie's attention by making a big show of reaching under the table, seemingly to grab something that wouldn't sit still.

"What is it?" Katie asked.

"I can't hold it back any longer," he said. He brought his hands up as if he were trying to contain a small, wild animal. Katie's alarm vanished when he opened his hands and presented the pipe to her along with a tin box of Lucifer matches.

"You bought me a nose warmer!"

"To thank you for your words," he said, chuckling. "They're singing our song about poor old Robert Partridge in all the pubs." His smile was broad and handsome.

"I'm glad, but I gave those lines to stop your cursing. You were a misery to be with for a week and more."

"My muse was on holiday. I *was* miserable."

Katie smiled. "I should be jealous."

"No, Katie," Conway said with all seriousness. "I write grim ballads, as you know. My muse is an old hag with tits that sag so low she must tie them in a knot and throw them over her shoulder to keep from stepping on them. She is good for tales of woe, but that's all."

47

Katie giggled at the image and Conway grinned.

"Now that you have the cuttie," he said gesturing to his gift, "you have no reason to steal *my* pipe."

Yes, but then a new way would have to be found to grab his attention.

~ ~ ~

When they were not traveling or otherwise engaged in chapbook production or sales, they both worked for Conway's cousin, a man named William Hargis. Katie worked as a scourer for Hargis' wife, Mary, who ran a laundry. Conway worked for Hargis on a team of night soil men. Gone most of the night, he'd return close to dawn, reeking of aged human feces. The pay for the work was good and frequently included a bottle of gin. Conway poured the gin in his bath water to help remove the smell of feces. The surplus, he sold to a local publican.

Katie worked harder day to day than ever before. The rewards were clear. For the first time in her life, she found she could frequently eat her fill.

"I love your bones, but I don't miss them." Conway told her. "You look good with a round bosom."

Katie blushed. She was pleased to think she was taking on a more attractive form. Attractive people had an easier time in life. Attractive women could become music hall singers.

If only I could persuade him of the need to dress the part. Conway knows he must dress well to make his sales, but he's content to wear secondhand and readymades.

With time, Conway came to consider her his common law wife. Katie welcomed the new role and had his initials tattooed on her left arm.

A Portion of a Pair of Spectacles

Katie met a neighbor on a warm summer Saturday while hanging clothes to dry in the rear of the tenement. She had climbed a ladder to use the clothes line that stretched across the thin alley to the building on the other side. A woman, a bit older than Katie, with dark brown hair and a sallow complexion, was hanging clothes on a line outside a window higher up on the building across the way. She paused while hanging a shirt and leaned out of the window and waved her free hand. "Good afternoon. I'm Anne. I live up there with my husband, George Bray." She pointed straight up, and swayed a bit as if she were dizzy. Katie gasped as Anne caught herself before falling out of the window.

The woman seemed unafraid, and that inspired a humorous thought: *Anne and her husband live on top of the building, on the sloped roof, and their furniture is always tipping over and tumbling to the ground.* A foolish fantasy, yet beyond the fence surrounding the building's back lot, a broken chair squatted amidst weeds.

"I'm Kate." She wasn't sure why she said it like that, but it sounded more adult than *Katie* and felt good. She gestured toward her building. "I live with my husband..." she liked the sound of that too "...just here."

"Good to meet you."

"And you," Katie said.

Anne ducked back into the building and was gone. Katie went on with her work, only to be startled when Anne spoke directly below her. "That looks hard, having to climb the ladder with your wash."

"It isn't too bad." Katie had become soaked from hauling the wash up in batches, hung over her shoulders. "You don't live on the roof, do you?"

"No." They both laughed. "We're in the attic room." Anne lifted a pair of trousers from Katie's tub and handed them up to her. "My husband is looking for work," she said, her words slightly slurred. "He were a market porter, but hurt his back. You hear of anything without lifting, you let me know." She handed Katie a couple of blouses and that was the last of it. "I work for the Lucifer Company, making matches."

Katie climbed down. "Conway is my husband's name. He's a chapman. I hawk his chapbooks with him."

"Chapbooks shan't do me any good—I can't read!" Anne laughed again and leaned heavily against the building. She was indeed unsteady. "My husband could read to me, but he's got a terrible stutter. It'd c-c-c-ome out all br-br-br-broken."

Katie laughed along with her. "Perhaps I could teach you to read."

"All that, just to sell a chapbook?" Anne smiled crookedly, then touched her jaw. "Damned tooth." She reached for a flask in the pocket of her apron and took a drink from it. "Please excuse me," she said. "I haven't been myself. I don't make a habit of drinking. I'd offer you some, but it's really just for my tooth ache."

"I don't—" Katie started to say. She turned away from Anne and gaze down the alley. "I-I've never had a drink." She smiled sheepishly.

"Then I'll have to make the introduction sometime."

"Perhaps." Katie said without conviction.

"Very good to meet you," Anne said and turned back toward her building.

"Yes, and you."

Anne stumbled over a loose paving stone crossing the alley, caught herself and continued into the building. Katie returned to her room and the afternoon's work.

~ ~ ~

She asked Conway to call her Kate. He agreed, but she had to remind him so often, she eventually gave up on it.

She saw Anne frequently after that, usually on a Saturday, a day they both found time for the wash. Despite the woman's constant mouth pain, she was humorous and Katie enjoyed laughing with her.

Conway didn't hide his contempt for Anne when Katie told him she spent time with the woman. "I've seen her drunk and I know her kind," he said.

"She drinks because of a toothache. When that's gone, I'm certain she'll be quite respectable."

"She has the match maker's curse," Conway said. "She'll not be getting better."

Katie didn't want to hear that. She decided Conway had invented the curse to make Anne undesirable. But she didn't argue with him, and she avoided going to the rear of the building during the time when she regularly saw Anne.

Scornful of anyone who drank, Conway disdained her association with most everyone, making it difficult for her to have friends. The women from the laundry where Katie worked met on Tuesday nights at a pub to have a few pints, sing songs, and make idle talk. Katie was invited, but Conway said, "If you go to the pub, you'll take up drinking and I'll have to turn you out in the street."

Katie had an urge to take a drink of spirits to spite him. She could hide one of the bottles of gin he brought home, so she could try it when he was gone. What could he do? He needed her. *But it's foolish to look for trouble. S*he put the idea out of her head.

Katie wanted to get away from him for a while at times, but Conway kept her close when she was not at work and insisted she turn her wages over to him. "Your earnings," he said, "should be saved against future need."

In these matters, her feelings and opinions were obviously of no consequence to Conway. The shine was off the man and dark clouds began to form in their relationship. She truly had next to nothing in the world that didn't belong to Conway.

In response, Katie did two things: She decided to bring home from the laundry mending work for which she'd receive extra pay, and she started keeping her mother's thimble on her person at all times. On the occasions she felt troubled, she'd stick her finger inside the thimble to touch the bright silver, thereby "touching" her mother. When she brought home the mending work, she told Conway it was all part of her work for Mary Hargis so he'd assume it was included when she handed over her earnings. The extra pay "under the table," as it were, didn't amount to much, but over time it would accumulate into enough to buy some fine clothes.

The baseboard in the corner behind their bed, was split into two pieces. She'd discovered that the smaller piece, about a foot long, right in the corner, was not held in place so much as wedged in. Behind it the wooden lath was broken away, revealing a small space within the wall. Perhaps a previous tenant had used it as a hiding place. The piece of baseboard fit in place neatly and she might never have discovered it if she hadn't kicked it while making the bed. The space held nothing, and Katie was fairly certain Conway was unaware of it. She decided to hide her savings there in a tin match box.

One Saturday, she stayed home to do their laundry, while Conway went to see his printer. Going up and down the ladder to the clothes line in the hot and muggy air left her winded and she sat and rested with her back against the building.

The window Anne used to access her clothes line was shut.

A slight breeze blew against Katie's wet laundry, then hit the wall of the building and flowed down over her, bring with it cooling air. She wiped the sweat from her forehead and neck and enjoyed the sensation. *I might see Anne, should I wait a while.*

Katie loaded her cuttie and lit it. As she smoked, the wind shifted and the alley began to heat up. The hot smoke from her pipe became biting and bitter in the warm air. She snuffed it out and was about to get up and go inside when a door opened across the way and Anne emerged. She moved slowly and in an awkward, bent manner.

"I saw you through the window and thought to give you something what belonged to my mother," Anne said, her words slurred perhaps because of the tooth ache, but more likely because of drunkenness. She sat down next to Katie. Her clothing was soaked through with sweat.

From the pocket of her apron, she produced half a pair of spectacles and offered them to Katie. "They were broken," she said. "I couldn't find the other half, but when I do, I'll bring them to you and you can mend them."

"I couldn't take them from you," Katie said. "You might need them."

"You're not taking them," Anne said. "I'm giving them to you. I have no problem with my eyes. Should you read much, you'll harm your eyes without spectacles. As what my mum always said. I don't read and George will never wear them."

"Thank you," Katie said. She slipped them into the pocket with her thimble.

Anne leaned back against the building and let out a deep sigh. "It's so hot, and the air has been foul."

"Were foul air and evil vapors killed my mum," Katie said.

"I'm tempted to lie on the paving stones in the shade. They must be cooler than my bed."

As ill as Anne appeared to be, her suggestions was more alarming still. Katie always checked back lanes before entering them. "You mustn't stay in the alley. Young bludgers move through here."

Anne nodded her head absently.

Mine must be cooler than Anne's attic room. She could come lie on my bed for a while. Katie almost made the suggestion, but held her tongue, knowing that Conway would become angry if he came home to find the drunken woman in his bed.

Anne took a sip from her flask and offered it to Katie.

She hesitated only a moment, then took a deep draught. The sour liquor burned her mouth and throat in a manner so unpleasant she regretted it instantly and decided never to take a drink again.

Is that what it always tastes like, or did I drink from an elixir what's harming Anne?

Is she cursed as Conway said? Is she sick from drink? Now that I've had the drink, will I be cursed or become ill?

If Conway finds out, he'll leave me in the street.

She tried to relax and let the questions go.

Nothing will come of it if I have no more. He'll never find out.

As they sat silently for a time, a warm spot grew in Katie's belly and slowly spread throughout her body. She found herslf soothed in an odd way as her troubles, both physical and mental tensions, left her. Carried for a lifetime, the troubles went largely unnoticed, like a burden in a rucksack, accumulated slowly, consistently over a journey of many miles. The relief created by their sudden absence was spellbinding.

This is not a bad thing. Conway can't always know what I'm doing. There must be times when I decide for myself.

Anne interrupted her dreamy state, "I'll return to my room and lie down." She got up, and reached for the flask still in Katie's hand.

"No," Katie heard herself say, drawing back with the flask. She didn't want to be separated from it.

Anne's eyes narrowed a little, her brow tightened, and she opened her mouth to speak. Katie cut her off.

"May I have another drink before you go?"

Anne nodded her head and Katie took a painful gulping pull off the flask and handed it back nearly empty. Anne shook it with a worried look in her eyes, but said nothing. Wiping her burning mouth on the back of her hand and feeling a touch of regret for taking so much, Katie watched Anne turn and make her way slowly back into her building.

I'm sure she has more back in her room, Katie told herself, and the feeling that she'd stolen the poor woman's medicine went away.

She returned with the empty wash tub to her room. Five of Conway's bottles of gin stood beside a cake of soap and a flannel on a shelf near the wash tub. Katie took one and hid it with her savings behind the baseboard in the corner by the bed. The hiding place was large enough that she was able to slide it behind the secured piece of baseboard. Even if the short piece were kicked loose, the bottle couldn't be seen.

That is what I shall save against future need.

As her intoxication deepened, she lay on the bed. Without a care in the world, she willingly fell into the calming, euphoric state. She slept through the remaining daylight hours and was awaken by Conway's return.

"You didn't finish your work," he said, shaking her by the foot. "I asked you to fold those broadsheets together."

"I'm...sorry." Katie hoped she didn't sound as groggy as she felt. "I didn't mean to fall asleep. You know I've been ill in the mornings lately. This afternoon, I were ill again and had to lie down."

Katie got up and moved to take the wash off the line. She held a terrible secret, one that was as harmful as it was delightful.

Conway gave no indication that he was on to her.

~ ~ ~

Anne's toothache never went away. The few times Katie saw her after the day she was given the partial spectacles, Anne was in increasingly worse condition. Most of her teeth fell out and her jaw became abscessed. Within a few months she was dead.

Did I hasten Anne's death by drinking her medicine? The thought reminded her of the times she upset her mother while Catherine was ill and dying. Katie tried to be numb to the loss. Anne was not completely gone, after all, since Katie still had her gift. She liked to think that one day, Anne would find the other half of the spectacles and bring it to her.

Katie hoped Anne's curse would not be visited upon her, but suspected she now had a curse of her own. Although the notion removed the temptation to drink, she would keep the hidden bottle of gin for herself out of defiance.

A Pair of Brown Stockings with Mended Feet

While at home in the winter of 1865, Katie began to suffer a dull ache in her back and lower abdomen, pressure on her pelvis, and her belly became hard, all at dreadful intervals. The periods of time between the combined pain and pressure, when her belly relaxed, were becoming shorter.

Katie didn't want to go to the workhouse infirmary, but she knew that was where Conway had planned for her to have the baby all along. Her fear of the place kept her from admitting that the infant was on the way until almost too late.

"You can't have your babe at home," Conway said. "If it goes badly, I cannot help you. Everyone knows the infirmary at the workhouse is for lying in too. How many women use it for just that? You know you'll be fine."

He put her in her coat and bonnet, donned his own coat and hat, and ushered her out the door and into the cold and damp winter air. Trying to walk up the lane, they quickly faced the obvious truth that Katie wouldn't be able to walk to the workhouse fast enough.

Mr. Pettit was returning home from market with his gaily painted coster's barrow. Conway hailed him and asked for the use of the cart.

"I've still got half a barrel of pickled whelks," Mr. Pettit said. "I'll take them home and return with the cart."

"There's no time," Conway said with urgency.

Another bout of pain and pressure caused Katie to cringe and let out a moan.

"Yes, I see," Mr. Pettit said, nodding his head. "I shall take the whelks with me. Let's get her comfortable."

Mr. Pettit removed a small barrel and a drum, then he and Conway helped Katie climb into the cart, allowing her to rest her back against a pile of empty canvas sacks that smelled of smoked fish.

"Good luck," he said, and Conway began pushing Katie in the cart through the deepening dark.

"I'm afraid you'll leave me there," Katie said, her voice more pitiful than she intended, as it bumped along with the cart over uneven paving stones.

"And lose my best patterer?" Conway said, his words puffing out plumes of vapor. "I wouldn't sell half the ballads if you weren't there to show them how it's done."

When they arrived, Conway helped her out of the cart. "You must make your own way from here. Should they be short of beds and see you have a husband, they shan't take you in."

"No, I can't stay here alone."

"You'll not be alone. There are nurses to help you along. You'll see."

Katie clung to Conway.

"I can't leave Mr. Pettit's coster barrow in the street."

Katie gave him a cold look. *No, but you've threatened to leave me in the street.*

He kissed her on the head and turned her toward the building's entrance. "In you go," he said, as if talking to a frightened child. "I'll come back tomorrow."

Katie took a step toward the grim brick building. The cart's wheels made a grinding sound as Conway turned it. She glanced back to see that he already headed south along the lane.

Two elderly inmates acting as nurses greeted her inside the building. Their faces held no expression. They led Katie into a long, thin, high-ceilinged room filled with beds occupied by women of different ages, in various states of awareness. The stares from some of the inmates became disquieting. The odors were odd.

The matrons found her a bed and put screens around it to provide privacy. Katie kicked off her shoes, exposing her tattered stockings. Seeing them, one of the matrons left and returned shortly to offer Katie a pair of brown ribbed stockings that had been mended with white yarn.

"Thank you," she said. The woman, still expressionless, turned away from her without a word. Katie felt some relief when the two matrons left her, but worried they might not be available when she needed help.

The straw mattress was thin and the room so cold and drafty, Katie took only her coat and bonnet off before getting in the bed. She located her thimble in an outer pocket and slipped a finger into it.

Katie heard distant conversations, but made no effort to understand what was said. Some of the words sounded casual and thoughtful. A quiet ranting came from someone who might have been senile or insane. An inmate in a nearby bed kept up a low moaning, while another across the room periodically cried out in pain. Through a crack between the screens a woman could be seen conversing with an unseen companion.

She allowed the activity to take her mind off the intermittent pain and pressure as much as possible, yet within a short time further distraction became impossible.

Katie named her baby girl, Anne, but she and Conway called her Annie. Many of the women in the neighborhood came to visit the infant. Conway complained, but Katie put him in his place. "If you expect me to hawk chapbooks in the street with you, Annie had better makes friends among the neighbors."

Fortunately, Annie was a charming, cooing baby who made friends with everyone she met. She didn't cry often and was easily amused. For Katie, Annie seemed a flawless replica of what she had been in youth, with her delicate toes and fingers, velvet-soft skin, dark silken hair, and jewel-bright blue eyes that with time turned green. She represented a chance to start over—what would be Annie's would be Katie's. The infant would grow strong and whole and have a good life. Her mother might be a music hall singer. Her father would not die and leave the family in abject poverty. She would grow up and marry a proper gentleman who earned a good wage. They would have a large and loving family, all of them educated, well-fed, healthy, and happy. In Katie's declining years, Annie would embrace her and keep her, providing a comforting respite from all of life's hard work. Old age would be tolerable. She would be let down easily and gently, and finally join Catherine in peace.

But that was in the future. For now, there was work to do. Little time passed before Katie got back on her feet and had several neighborhood women willing to spell her when she needed a little time away from her infant. Conway kept a list of them. If he ever saw one of the women drunk, she was scratched off his list and Annie would not be seeing her again.

Conway wanted Katie to return to work at the laundry, and hired a childminder, Mrs. Patricia Ennis, to keep Annie throughout the workday. Unhappy to be allowing a stranger to take care of her infant, Katie nevertheless delivered Annie to the childminder on a Wednesday morning in early spring.

The wooden house had a sagging roof with holes and a broken chimney pot puffing smoke unevenly. The old woman who answered the door reached for Annie without introduction.

"I'll carry her in," Katie said.

"Surname?" The woman asked.

"Conway," Katie said. "And you are Mrs. Ennis?"

"Yes."

Perhaps in her seventies, Mrs. Ennis appeared to be all gray; her hair, her clothes, her complexion, and expression. An old-fashioned bonnet with ties at the chin sat askew on her head. She turned stiffly and led the way, mounting the stairs to the second floor. At the top of the stairs, they came to a short dark hall which served as a storage area. A thin path for walking had been cleared between heaps of various household items and building supplies that included bricks. The path branched to provide access to doors on both sides of the hall. The smell of fresh, as well as old feces and urine grew strong as they entered a room on the right that held numerous infants in crude cribs.

Eight of the cots were occupied. At least ten more were not. No wondered the woman was too distracted for introductions. Katie presumed that the empty cribs would be filled as infants were delivered by their mothers.

Bedding in the cribs was soiled and the walls and floor were bespattered. The ceiling needed repair of damage from roof leakage. A haze of fireplace smoke hung in the air.

"Put her anywhere," Mrs. Ennis said, moving to a table in the corner and picking up a small, tapered bottle containing a small amount of dark liquid.

Katie didn't want to put Annie down. She moved toward the corner because the table appeared somewhat clean.

Mrs. Ennis pulled the cork from the bottle, measured out a spoonful of the liquid and fed it to the nearest infant.

"Is the poor child ill?" Katie asked.

"No ma'am," she said, moving on to the next infant in the row. "This keeps them quiet. I give it to all of them. They sleep through the day and are bright and happy when their mums come for them in the evening."

An empty bottle of the elixir sat on the table. Katie picked it up and read the label.

Godfrey's Cordial
For a child 1 month old—4 or 5 drops
For a child 2 month old—7 drops
For a child 3 month old—10 drops
For a child 6 month old—20 drops
For a child 12 month old—half a teaspoonful
Shake well

"The label on the bottle says it is to be given in drops, not spoonfuls," she said with urgency.

"Yes, Ma'am," Mrs. Ennis said. "I measured out only half the spoon."

Katie tried to watch her more carefully the next time she dosed an infant, but the woman turned away as she began to pour.

She puts them to sleep so she doesn't have the bother of keeping them happy.

Mrs. Ennis held up the empty bottle. "I'll have to get more." She set the bottle and gray metal spoon on the table next to Katie and left the room, moving unsteadily.

She acts as if she's taking the medicine too.

Katie set the bottle back down. She took the teaspoon from the table and slipped it in a pocket. *The medicine is probably harmless, but perhaps she'll have a harder time giving it to the children without a spoon.*

She turned with Annie to leave as one of the infants began to cry.

No doubt she'll find another spoon. Katie hurried down the stairs. She exited the building and didn't look back, knowing she'd just fought the first in a long series of battles to protect Annie. The next one would be with Conway. Unless he was willing to keep Annie, Katie would not be going to work today. Whatever the case, Conway would not be pleased.

Katie took the long way home through Covent Garden Market to see the new domed Floral Hall that replaced a part of the old arcade. Although still under construction, it was already a beautiful steel and glass building. The Covent Garden Market, a bloodless market where only products of the garden and orchard were sold, smelled good. New vegetables had not come in yet, but flowers of every hue were in abundance. Katie breathed deeply of their combined fragrance. The costermongers were on their best behavior as the proper ladies, in their finery, bought things they didn't need.

One day Annie shall buy flowers here.

A young Irish girl with pale orange hair approached Katie. "Please ma'am, a farthing to carry your beautiful baby while you shop."

She had a pretty face and a trusting smile. She gazed at Annie with an innocent longing that made Katie proud to be the infant's mother. Her back was sore and she needed to trust someone, a stranger. Conway had given her a few pence so she wouldn't be on the street without money. He'd ask for it back later or want to know how it was spent, but she could always replace what was missing with some of her savings. "I'll give you ha'penny to carry her a mile," she said.

The girl's eyes became large and she grinned. "My name is Aisling," she said, reaching cautiously for the infant.

Katie tucked in Annie's swaddling and lowered her into Aisling's arms. They set off for home.

~ ~ ~

Conway was seated at the table, going through a stack new chapbooks when Katie and Annie returned. "You brought her home?" he said, clearly outraged. "You are daft as a brush, woman. You know you cannot work with the child in your arms. There must be a time when you are prepared to put her down."

"The childminder was a mistake," Katie said as calmly as possible, putting Annie in the bed.

Conway stood and raised his voice. "The mistake is that you think we can get along on my income alone."

Annie began to cry.

Katie leaned in toward Conway and said evenly, "Mrs. Ennis acted lke she was drunk. She were giving the children a medicine, Godfrey's Cordial."

Conway's eyes became wide, his nostrils flared and his lips

pulled back from his gritted teeth. He balled his fists and Katie cringed. "Opium and alcohol!" he shouted, turning away from Katie toward Annie. "That elixir kills children. It's been in the courts. It should be outlawed! Mrs. Ennis should be hanged."

Annie's crying became louder.

"I didn't know!" Katie said, fearing he might find a way to blame her and lash out with his fists, "but I couldn't leave Annie with her."

"No... no, you were right to bring her home." His voice had softened. He gently took Annie from the bed. As he held her close, she became quieter.

Conway seemed confused, frightened, as if he knew he'd made a terrible mistake hiring the childminder and didn't know how to make it right again. His eyes cast about restlessly. Katie had never seen him that way before. "She'll be lucky if she never hears from me," he blustered in a powerless whisper.

Katie's fear of Conway fled and she turned to him, speaking with authority. "We shall not leave Annie with another childminder. I will stay home with her when you work by day. When you don't work in the daytime, I'll go to the laundry."

His eyes clouded with regret, Conway nodded his approval.

She had not expected him to acquiesce so easily. He clearly loved his daughter. Perhaps Annie would indeed have a good future.

~ ~ ~

Katie returned to the laundry to work for a few weeks. Conway did what he could to find local women willing to care for Annie while he slept by day. But he couldn't always find one, and complained that his sleep was too frequently interrupted by Annie. Within a short time, he'd had his fill of the arrangement and allowed Katie to stay home.

When they traveled to an execution, Annie stayed with Charlotte Neet, a woman in her late sixties who lived nearby in the rookery of Old Pye Street. Katie had recommended her to Conway because she'd worked with Charlotte at the Hargis Laundry and thought she could be relied upon.

"She's not like so many at the laundry who drink their lunch,"

Katie told him. "She says she takes home a pint in a pale from a pub near her home and drinks it in the evening after her supper for 'good health.'"

Conway had a look of skepticism.

"She's a delight to be with as she's always smiling. We like to sing together while we're working. She's taught me some old songs. Charlotte's hands aren't strong enough to wash clothes anymore, but she can take care of Annie. She'll do it for a half-shilling per day."

Katie took Conway to see Charlotte. She lived in what had once been the pantry in a drafty, leaking house a quarter of a mile to the Southwest. At one time the house had no doubt held one family. With so little room in the old pantry, Katie and Annie stayed in the hall while Conway went in, shut the door, and spoke to Charlotte. Seeing a chamber pot and makeshift bed at her feet, Katie knew that she stood in the dwelling place of another tenant. Charlotte said the house had thirty-two tenants altogether.

Katie tried to hear what Conway and Charlotte said, but their voices were too muffled behind the door.

On their way home, Conway said, "Sixpence is a dear price, but she doesn't have the income from keeping a full nursery. I suppose it's worth it to leave Annie in trusted hands."

~ ~ ~

In 1868, executions ceased to be public events. Although hangings retreated behind the walls of prisons, crowds still gathered outside the prison gates to read the posting of the death notice and celebrate or protest the executions. Katie and Conway sold chapbooks at these events, but because the crowds weren't as large and there was less of a festival atmosphere, sales suffered. Katie's singing to attract customers became more important than ever. That pleased her.

Conway dipped more and more frequently into his savings to support the family. Katie thought of it as getting paid at long last, her wages invested in something she felt good about: the welfare of her daughter. Nothing would be left over to provide Katie with fine clothes and the dream that came along with them, but she was content. Her second chance to live had been well started.

~ ~ ~

In the autumn of 1870, Katie read in the London Gazette that Parliament had passed the Elementary Education Act that funded schools for all children ages five to twelve. She was so excited about it, she read the article to Conway.

"The charity schools did a good enough job for you," was his only response.

Annie was five years old that winter and began her education at the St. Marylebone School in the spring. Walking her daughter to school in the mornings took her in the direction of the Hargis Laundry. After delivering Annie to St. Marylebone, Katie went to work.

Conway was pleased with the extra income. The couple got along better than they had for a long time, until the day Katie told him she was pregnant again. After that, days passed when Conway would not speak unless spoken to. Over the course of her pregnancy, he became more distant.

Katie relished the times when he was away working with the night soil men. On those evenings, she helped Annie with her reading and writing lessons, giving her skills well beyond those of her classmates at the St. Marylebone School. With her daughter's language skills rapidly developing, Katie taught her to play word games. The first was *I'm Thinking of Something*, which was simple enough for a young girl, the questions involved requiring only *yes* and *no* answers.

Charlotte visited one evening while Conway was working. She'd come to play games with Katie and Annie and share a meal of potatoes and broxy. Charlotte said she hadn't had meat in over a month.

After supper, Annie said. "I want to wash up the dishes."

Katie would have to clean up later, but allowed her little girl to stand at the wash tub and make a mess. While Annie played in the soapy water, Katie and Charlotte shared jokes and had a smoke.

"How grand that you live in such a nice, clean home," Charlotte said with a loving smile and a warm grip on Katie's hands. "And to have lived here for so long—ten years! How welcoming it must be to walk through the door each day."

Indeed, it was the nicest home Katie had ever had. She smiled, feeling fortunate.

The three had fun playing games late into the night, then slept together in the bed until dawn when Conway returned. Charlotte got up and let herself out as he prepared to bathe. Eventually, he got in the bed.

~ ~ ~

With time, Annie had a good enough grasp of the alphabet that Katie introduced her to *Grandmother's Trunk*. "It were my favorite game to play with my mother, your grandmother, Catherine."

"Where is Catherine?" Annie asked.

"She's gone now," Katie said, "died when I were just a girl. Your uncle Christopher thinks she plays *Grandmother's Trunk* with people in heaven."

Annie smiled at the idea, then changed the opening line for the game. "My grandmother, Catherine, has a trunk." She beamed at her mother as if she'd surprised herself with her own cleverness. "In it was an ape!" Annie giggled so long and hard, she fell over backwards out of the bed. After a loud thump, came a silent pause in which Katie's heart caught in her throat. She hurried to help, but by the time she reached her daughter, Annie was giggling again. Laughing, they fell together, hugging.

From then on, the game was known to them as *Catherine's Trunk*. Whenever Annie had a hard time choosing an object, she'd say, "I have to ask Catherine what's next." She'd turn to one side and pretend to consult her grandmother, then listen as if Catherine were whispering in her ear.

That seemed to bring Catherine back to life, in part because Annie possessed a mischievous sense of humor much like that of Katie's mother.

~ ~ ~

Conway became increasingly irritable while trying to write, which he currently did at home, since Katie cooked their meals to save the expense of eating at the tavern.

He could not hear conversation and think of words to write at the same time. "In the tavern, the hubbub of voices has no meaning," he explained. "But at home, should I hear one clear voice, I can't help but think about what's said. It breaks my thoughts. I can't have that." On the occasions when someone did speak while he wrote, he became cross. Katie and Annie were obliged to find something to do that required no talking.

One night he was unusually restless. While he sat at the table, working on a ballad, Katie and Annie played a game of Jackstraws; one of several *quiet* games they played in the evenings when Conway was working. Annie won a round of the game and let out a tiny giggle.

Making a show of having his thoughts interrupted, Conway sat back in his chair and loaded his pipe. "I'm not blaming you for the poor quality of the ballads," he said to Katie, "but sales for the last two would have been better if I'd depended solely upon myself."

He was talking about money, not ballads, and Katie knew better than to respond. She and Annie started a new round of Jackstraws.

Conway leaned forward again and began to write. He grumbled and cursed, scratched out lines, wadded the paper angrily, then carefully smoothed it back out.

Finally, he shouted, "This room is a *cage*!" He grabbed his coat and hat and fled out into the night.

"Is Papa angry with me?" Annie asked.

"No, he's angry with himself," Katie said. "If he were a different man, I should worry about him. But he's not."

"I don't understand," Annie said.

"That's all right," Katie said. "You're not meant to." She tousled the girl's hair and smiled. "He'll be back soon. He's never had anywhere to go at night."

~ ~ ~

Katie wasn't frightened to go to the workhouse to give birth in 1871. As the pressure suddenly began to increase on her lower pelvis, she knew the time was approaching and was determined to be in the lying-in ward before labor began.

When Conway delivered her to the workhouse, he said, "Give

me a boy this time so I can put him to work."

Katie's eyes blazed. "Have you been thinking of sending Annie out to find work?

"No, she is too young," Conway said, his face set and his eyes narrowed.

"If I give you a son today, he would not be able to work for at least ten years, except in the cruelest and worst conditions."

"I don't mean to send my children to work in the mines."

Katie didn't like his dismissive tone. "You know there is education for all children now, ages five to twelve."

"I was educated until I was ten," Conway said, disgust in his voice, "and as you know, that has served me well."

"You'll not be putting Annie to work in four years!" Katie said, struggling to keep from spitting the words. "If she's to have a good life, she must have a full education." She lowered the volume and pitch of her voice to make sure Conway felt the threat in it and said, "I will do whatever I have to do to make sure of that."

Conway glared back at her for a moment, then said, "I'll not stand in the street and argue." He turned on his heels and headed for home.

Katie took deep breaths, allowing her anger to dissipate in the cool evening air.

She checked her pockets and located her thimble before making her way into the building.

Two Unbleached Calico Pockets

Katie had a boy. She didn't feel as attached to him as she had been to Annie when she was first born, but assumed that would change with time.

Conway named him Thomas, and clearly didn't look upon the boy as mere chattel. Indeed, he was so delighted to have a son, his recent bad temper faded for a time. He cooed and tickled the boy. He sang "This is the Way the Ladies Ride" and bounced him gently on his knee. "Look at the smiles he gives his papa. He has your good looks, but my humor."

Surely he would not be able to send Thomas off to work when he became ten years old. Perhaps he would not be willing to cut Annie's childhood short either. Katie was glad his good humor had returned. Their room was too crowded for such unhappiness. Thomas slept with the adults. Annie had a small child's bed of her own.

Conway shared in the duties of getting up and down in the night for the first months. The assistance was more than he'd provided when Annie had been an infant. Katie was grateful for the help since Thomas made a mess of his nappy at every opportunity. She sewed two new calico pockets to wear under her top skirt so she could carry extra nappies, a flannel, and other infant needs while not at home.

With Annie making her own way to school, walking the two miles with friends, Katie could stay home with Thomas.

One afternoon, while Conway was off meeting a new printer, Katie went to the fish market to buy eel. They'd had little but potatoes for several days and she'd been feeling weak. She set out, carrying Thomas in his swaddling within a loop of calico supported on her left shoulder. He was cranky until she shifted him a couple times and got him settled. Katie walked the mile and a half to market in a little less than an hour, along narrow streets and lanes, past houses shuttered against the bitter air, past shops with doors wide open and shopkeepers shouting slogans to the street from within, past publicans with their large lamps lit and glowing begrudgingly within the bright, hazy air.

She came upon a group of people clustered around a child crying at the kerb. The little girl pointed to a drain. "I dropped the penny Mum give me to buy the family supper. She'll beat me for making us go hungry." A laborer took pity on the child and gave her a coin.

At the market, shuffling along, at times shoulder to shoulder with other customers, moving from one fish cart to the next, Katie became nauseated by the closeness and the foul odors. She stepped away into more open air, where the human traffic thinned but swirled in a more chaotic manner, and was startled to happen upon her sister, Emma.

She had been swallowed up by the workhouse so long ago— Katie had not thought much of her sister's chances of surviving the experience and coming out of it a whole human being. As with the last time they'd seen each other, Katie got the odd impression she faced a ghost, but one who now stood before her healthy, soberly dressed, and with color in her cheeks.

Barely aware of the people flowing around them in the market, Katie approached to touch Emma's cheek. Her dark hair had a bit of gray at the temples. Her features had lost their softness, her skin looking somewhat coarse.

Emma smiled warmly. Noticing Thomas, her smile grew larger still, revealing gaps in her teeth.

"This is your nephew, Thomas," Katie said, smiling through unaccountable distress at the chance meeting. Then she understood: She'd been gripped by shame for having not communicated with her sisters and brother for so long.

Watching her sister gently stroke Thomas's cheek, she knew there was no reason for the shame. Certainly, Emma held no hard feelings. Love still held them together. With that, Katie had a sudden longing to see Margaret and Christopher.

"He's beautiful," Emma said. "Mr. Matthews and I have not been blessed with children."

"The gentleman you met at the workhouse?"

"Yes, we were married five years ago. He's now a master-lumper

70

under a publican in Bermondsey. Most of what they unload are the ships hauling timber. I work for a trotter boiler. We have a good life, but it could be better." Emma shrugged and smiled tightly.

Work at the trotter boilers, peeling the fur from the scalded sheep's feet, was hard toil. Remembering the state they were in when Emma picked oakum in the workhouse, Katie looked at her sister's prematurely aged hands.

Emma anticipated her. "I'm an overseer. I were on my way to visit one of the girls what works under me. She's staying with her mother after having a baby of her own, a girl."

"What have you heard from Christopher and Margaret?"

"Margaret is a spinster, living with us. Her health hasn't been the same since the Lump Hotel. When she can, she works with me."

Emma turned and looked toward the river and nearby docks before continuing. "When we were in the workhouse, we received a letter from Christopher saying he worked for a boot manufacturer in Bermondsey, but he didn't say what company and we never found him, nor anyone who knew much about him. A man I talked to at the Beckham Boot Company said that if it were the Christopher he knew, he thought the press gang got him and he died in the West Indies. But there's no way to know the truth of it."

"If he's abroad, I'm certain he's found a way to survive," Katie said. "Christopher is clever and capable."

She didn't want to believe her brother had died, but arguing against the mere idea of it felt foolish, so she changed the subject. "I'm glad to hear you and Mr. Matthews are doing well."

"And you?" Emma asked. "You have a family now."

Katie told her about Conway, of being turned out of Aunt Elizabeth's home, her life in Westminster and the chapman business. "Thomas is my second child," she said. "I hope you'll soon meet my oldest, Annie. She is so like our Mum." She shifted Thomas to her other hip, considering what more to tell Emma about her life, her feelings.

She wanted to tell her about all her frustrations with Conway, how cold and calculating he could be while appearing to be solicitous. She wanted to admit that she didn't have the same feelings for Thomas that she did for Annie. Katie wanted to explain that there were times when she could see the world through her daughter's eyes, when she knew what she was thinking and felt what Annie felt. Katie had kept all that to herself. As a pressure on her heart, she needed to express those things, but somehow she wasn't close enough to Emma to feel she could share them. Still, she needed to talk, and no telling when she would see Emma again.

"I work for the Hargis Laundry, run by Conway's cousin. Since Thomas was born, I've stayed home to care for him. Every couple of days I pick up the mending at the laundry and do it at home. But I need to work more. I'm afraid should our income not improve, Conway will want to send Annie out to work."

"How old is she?"

"Six."

"That's too young. Just a few more years and she'll be ready."

"No!" Katie stepped back to get a different view of her sister.

Emma's brow went up and she tilted her head, clearly not understanding Katie's reaction.

"She shall get a full education, as the new law allows," Katie said.

"The law is fine for some," Emma said, "but those who have need still send their children to work."

"That's just what I'm afraid Conway is thinking." Katie swallowed hard and took a deep breath. "There are some in Parliament who believe all children *must* go to school. They want to make it the law."

"Until then," Emma said, "quite reasonably, parents will choose depending on their needs."

"An education is important," Katie said.

"You finished school—has it helped you earn a better crust?"

Katie frowned as she thought about her life of menial labor. Her contributions to Conway's ballads—that had been something she might not have provided without an education. Some of those ballads had sold well.

But Emma shook her head emphatically, as if anticipating

Katie again.

"If you had children," Katie asked, "at what age would you send them out to work?"

"But I don't have children," Emma said, frowning.

"That is a cowardly answer," Katie said, raising her voice. "Pray tell, what age?"

"I cannot answer," Emma said, her voice curt and eyes fiery. "I shan't answer. It's not my place."

"You're lucky you won't have to." Katie didn't hide the disgust in her voice. "As I recall, when you were just a girl, you were a piecer at the cotton mill, working ten hours a day. Of all people, you should know what hard labor does to a child."

"What I *know* is that I would have nothing but misery if it weren't for Mr. Matthews." Emma spoke quickly, as if she needed to have her say before her emotions prevented her from putting the words together properly. "What I *know* is that women have little in this world and must allow their husbands to make these decisions. Don't jeopardize what you have. Don't fight your husband's will. It is not your place."

"A mouthy haybag is what you are," Katie said. "Can you not think for yourself?"

"How can you speak to me this way?" Emma's face was pinched with hurt instead of anger.

"How should I speak to you when you want my children sent off to work, but cannot say if you'd commit your own children to hard labor?" Katie knew she was too strident in her language and tone, even cruel, but it felt good, as if she were telling Conway what she thought.

"Please, Katie," Emma's lip quivered and she lowered her gaze to the pavement. "We haven't seen each other in so long. Don't let it be like this."

"It shouldn't be up to me how things are. You've made that clear."

Emma merely expressed conventional wisdom, but Katie couldn't help taking it personally. "Goodbye, Emma. Take good care of yourself." She turned and walked away from her sister.

"Please," Emma called out, but Katie ignored her.

She didn't feel good about her anger or the way she'd treated Emma. Because she didn't get her address, she might not see Emma or Margaret again for a long time, but pride kept her walking.

Trying not to think about it, Katie finished her errand and started for home.

I'd just about persuaded myself Conway loves his children too much to send them off to work. Wishful thinking. He thought much of the idea when he were penniless. When he feels the pinch again, he'll know, as I do, he's not alone—many take as a given that Annie should toil away her childhood, her health. I can't fight them all. I must choose my battles—it did no good to argue with Emma.

Katie came upon the little girl she'd seen earlier. Again, she cried about losing her penny, this time down a different drain. Katie understood the girl's fakement, but such cozening was better than laboring in some mill. She gave the child one of her precious pennies and moved on.

Thomas fussed and cried the rest of the way home. The reek of his soiled nappy rose up around her as she walked. The sun hugged the horizon as they arrived home. Annie would be back from school soon. Katie unlocked the padlock on the door and let herself in. Conway hadn't come home yet. Her back hurt. She put Thomas on the bed and changed his nappy. He still fussed and she knew he must be hungry. She lit a lamp and sat at the table to feed him. He always took her nipples too hard and she suspected that was part of why she didn't take to him the way she did Annie. A petty thing, if it were true, but she couldn't help it. When he was done, Katie placed him in the bed.

Reaching into the corner behind the bed, she removed the short piece of baseboard and pulled out the tin match box containing her savings and put the board back in place. She sat at the table and spilled the contents of the matchbox onto the surface.

Katie counted five pounds, sixteen shillings, eight pence— enough to buy a beautiful silk and velvet bodice, skirt and bonnet, the type of finery worn by an entertainer. Conway should understand her potential to make good money as a singer, but it all hinged on Katie being allowed to spend time in places where so many people became drunk. In the end, he would never permit it.

Understanding that and being reconciled to it, she made some decisions. *All will have to wait.* Her aspirations to be a professional singer would be delayed until after Annie had finished her education. She stirred the coins with her fingers. *Put these savings back into the household funds so Conway will be none the wiser. Stop holding back earnings from the Hargis Laundry.* Since staying home with Thomas, she'd been turning over half her extra earnings to Conway so he wouldn't think she worked for nothing. *Find more mending work and toil late into the night, every night, if need be. Return to work full-time when Thomas starts school.*

Katie lit her cuttie and puffed it to life, then reached for her silver thimble and rolled it in her rough, dry hands. They were the hands of a scourer, like her mother's.

The silver plate was long gone from the outside of the thimble.

Catherine's words chimed softly in her memory. "Take care you don't wear yourself out the way your poor mum has." Katie's mother had worked herself into an early grave at the age of forty, trying to take care of her children.

The warning was good to consider, but Katie had little choice— she had to do what she could to earn her daughter's keep. Thomas's future was too far off to worry about.

She turned the thimble to look within it, to see the bright silver she knew must still line the inside. The thin light from the lamp didn't provide enough illumination. She hadn't looked inside for many years and wondered why it seemed important now.

Her shoulders sagged and she thought of the euphoric feeling she'd had the day Anne gave her a draft of her liquor. She looked to the shelf where Conway stored his bottles, but it was empty. The bottle she'd pushed far back behind the baseboard would still be in its hiding place. She moved to the corner behind the bed, removed the piece of baseboard, grabbed the bottle of gin and returned with it to the table.

She felt the years in her joints, her muscles, her head, and heart. How wonderful it would be to let all that go, to feel the euphoria

again, to be relieved of all her troubles, and sink into that warm, carefree embrace.

She opened the bottle and the liquor's foul odor made her nose and eyes sting and water.

Katie imagined Conway walking in on her while she was drinking, the row they would have, ending in her being tossed out in the street. She revised it so that she got away with taking the drink, but then he smelled it on her breath. The quarrel and her eviction followed. In the next version, she went outside after dark to have her drink of gin. That happened in the alley behind her tenement, and, having become drunk, she was so free of concern, even for her own safety, she fell prey to bludgers that roamed the alleys at night, looking for victims. Safer places could be found to have her drink, but none were safe when she began to picture herself the way she saw others who drank; stumbling about, saying and doing anything that came to mind, throwing caution to the wind. Each scenario ended with her children being left unprotected by their mother.

Katie remembered more of Catherine's words: "Take good care of your family and there will always be something of beauty in your life, something sterling. That's what keeps me going."

Annie is the one that is good and pure. She imagined quicksilver coursing through her daughter's veins. Annie would keep her going.

Katie put the cork back in the bottle. She returned it to the shelf from which she'd taken it so long ago. She wiped tears from her eyes, then set about to prepare the eel for supper.

A Mustard Tin

In 1881, at the age of 39, Katie had become her mother. Stiffness and soreness visited the joints throughout her body, but particularly in her hands. She had lost several teeth. When standing, she moved slowly to prevent a periodic lightheadedness that could lead to becoming insensible. She frequently had difficulty catching her breath and suffered coughing spells. The spells weren't nearly as severe as those of her mother, but were a reminder of what Catherine had experienced. Memories of her impatience with her mother always gave her a chill. *It is the cold dirt of her grave I feel, and perhaps my own.*

Katie sat at the table in her room putting the finishing touches on a dress bodice for Annie. The open door let in the warm, late-spring daylight, and she had the pleasant, periodic distraction of watching people walk by. Her neck ached from holding her head just right to balance the partial spectacles on her head, but she needed them to do close work as her vision had suffered from working by lamplight in the windowless room for so many years. Annie was worth all the effort. She had grown to be a beautiful, confident young woman.

Although Parliament had not made education compulsory until 1880, and then only for ages five to twelve, Katie had succeeded in preventing Annie from having to seek employment as a laborer. Conway recently argued that since the girl was soon to become sixteen years old, she should start pulling her own weight, and he put her to work selling chapbooks with disastrous results. Currently she had few responsibilities, a situation that could not stand long without her father demanding she find work.

With the idea that out of sight, was out of mind, Katie insisted that Annie spend much of her time with Charlotte Neet. With Katie's help, the elderly woman had recently moved into the room directly above the one occupied by Katie and her family. Charlotte's son, Richard, had prospered in recent years and sent her a small sum of money for food and rent each month.

Annie had recently met a possible suitor, renewing hope that her future would be bright. Katie needed to buy her a little more time.

Returning from an errand, Annie entered the room. When Katie saw the big smile on her face, all of her accumulated fatigue, thoughts of fading health, and mortality fled.

"James has made it plain that he's not entertaining other women!" Annie said.

Referring to the man by his first name was extraordinary. He was such a formal fellow, she had always called him Mr. Phillips.

Annie shook Katie by the shoulder and her partial spectacles slipped. "You know what that means, don't you?"

"Yes," Katie said, "but I am not surprised Mr. Phillips is devoted to you."

"He wants to come here to meet you and Papa."

"You mustn't let him," Katie said. "When the time is right, we shall meet him out at a tavern for a meal or perhaps during an outing to Hyde Park."

Annie's smile faded. "We are *not* paupers," she said indignantly.

"No, but we cannot risk Mr. Phillips deciding you're beneath his station."

"He's not that sort of man."

"All in good time, Annie." Katie tied off her thread, cut it and set aside her needle and tin thimble. "Look at this. I've altered it to become a long polonaise with side poufs to compliment your blue linen skirt. I added fringe and dobbin what tore off a fine skirt damaged at the laundry. See how it matches the big bow over the bustle? Mr. Phillips will be most impressed."

"It's beautiful, Mum, but it's not the way I dress. If you keep putting me in finer and finer clothes, I'll lose him for the opposite reason—*he* will feel the upstart."

"They're just scraps from the laundry, clothes people forgot or no longer needed. It's my needle and thread what brings them back to life. Any woman with my experience could do the same. It isn't dishonest, but, even so, should it bring the two of you closer, so much the better."

"You've always wanted to sing while wearing the fine clothes of an entertainer," Annie said, clearly trying to change the subject. "Why don't you create your own from such scraps?"

"I can alter a piece here or there, but I'm not a seamstress like your Great-Aunt Elizabeth. And I'd need fine cloth."

A bumping sound came from behind the open door. Katie put her finger to her lips and made a quite shushing. Annie nodded, dropped the bodice on the bed, and threw a blanket over it. Katie stepped forward and opened the door a little further, revealing her ten-year-old son. He was filthy from scavenging the river. "What is my little mudlark doing?" she asked. "Are you eavesdropping, Thomas?"

"No, Mum," he said without looking up. "I was knocking the clods off my shoes before coming in."

The boy's shoes were caked and his clothes and bare skin smeared with mud. He held in his arms a reeking canvas sack in which he carried the things he found at the river. The sack bulged with numerous short lengths of rope, scraps of sodden leather and what looked like the top of an old, ragged boot. The family didn't earn much for what he gathered, but it did amount to something.

"Well, take them off and come in."

Thomas kicked his shoes off, picked them up, then entered the room and made his way carefully past his mother and sister. He passed through the makeshift door Conway had recently put in the rear wall to give access to a storage room the landlord had cleared out for their use. The small chamber, another windowless affair, belonged to Annie and Thomas and made life in the small dwelling so much easier for them all. Conway had gained the room for the price of mucking out the building's cesspit. He and Thomas had done the work themselves.

Katie waited until her son shut the door before she spoke. "I hope he didn't understand what he heard. Should fortune shine upon you and Mr. Phillips wants you for his wife, your father will not be pleased. If he thinks Mr. Phillips might take you away, he'll want to have a talk with him. It could spoil everything. Your father wants to depend on you to sell chapbooks with him, but we've had enough of that."

"I don't mind, really," Annie said. "It was not so frightening, and I am well now." She lightly rubbed the nearly healed six inch gash on her upper arm.

A month earlier, Conway had insisted that Annie take Katie's place selling chapbooks with him at a hanging at Newgate prison. "You are not young and attractive anymore," he had told Katie. "Annie cannot sing, but she'll turn heads. You know that's what we need. She'll do fine."

Conway's slight still stung a little.

"I too were attacked the first time I went with him, but the bludger didn't cut me so deeply." She showed the old scar on her wrist, then delicately caressed the wound on her daughter's arm. "I'm so sorry for this."

"I shouldn't have held onto the coins," Annie said, a troubled look in her eyes. "I'm sure he thought I had more."

"You'll not go with your father again. *I'll* go."

"Until Mr. Phillips decides, there's no reason not to help Papa."

"You shall honor my wishes. We won't argue about it." Katie gathered the dress bodice in the blanket and handed it to Annie. "Take this to Charlotte. She'll hide it away for you until you want to wear it. Bring the blanket back right away."

"Yes, mum."

Katie watched her step outside, then leaned out the door to see her daughter move gracefully along the thin footway to the right. Mrs. Palman, who also lived upstairs, stepped through the door that led up to Charlotte's room, and held it for Annie as she went in.

Katie shut the door, and set about to warm water.

Carrying a bundle of fresh clothes, Thomas emerged from the new room nearly naked and sat on the edge of the bed.

"I found something for you," he said with a slight frown. "I'll wash it up this time."

Katie and Thomas had never been close, but as he got older, he seemed to understand that wasn't natural. Lately, he made small, awkward efforts to be sweet to Katie, bringing her things from the befouled banks of the River Thames.

He's learned from Conway to win hearts by giving gifts.

Last week Thomas brought home a piece of driftwood. "It's shaped like a dragon," he said, presenting it to Katie with a smile.

Even his smile is borrowed from Conway.

The driftwood reeked of the river and the small creatures that had bored holes in it, but to save his feelings, Katie kept it for a while.

Three days passed before Conway had had enough of the smell. "This has got to go," he told Thomas. "It is such a wonderful dragon, it smells like one." He made a funny face, wrinkling up his brow and nose, and Thomas smiled uncertainly. "Come, let's throw it in the stove and see if it can breathe fire from its nose and mouth."

Thomas's smile grew larger and he looked to his mother to see if she approved. Katie nodded her head. Conway spent nearly an hour watching the wood go up in flames in the old Soyer stove, making up stories about the dragon and sharing them with the giggling boy.

He can be such a warm father, yet he charms Thomas into scavenging on the river.

Katie looked at the fresh cuts on Thomas's legs from his "mudlarking adventures," alongside older, larger scars from cuts that had festered before healing up. He'd also suffered numerous intestinal and digestive ailments since beginning his activities on the river a year earlier.

Conway had introduced the idea of scavenging as *adventure.* He told tales, tall ones no doubt, of exotic cargos spilled from ships returning from the Orient, Africa, and the West Indies.

"There was a boy, another Thomas," Conway told his son one evening, "who, with his friends, discovered gold and silver coins washed up on the bank of the river in a load of silk from India. The boys secretly invested their find. By the time they were grown, their investment had earned a great fortune. They used it to buy their own ship. Then they assembled a crew of their best friends and sailed the world."

Thomas liked the story. On his days off from school, he went to the river, at first alone, and later with a few friends.

Katie was afraid for the boy, but Conway said, "You must let him learn to be an enterprising young man."

The water warmed, Katie helped Thomas bathe in the wash tub. When he was nearly finished, he reached for something in the bundle of fresh clothes he'd set beside the tub. "I found this for you." He showed her a small metal box with a hinged lid. "It's hardly rusted." He dipped it in the water. Using soap, he cleaned it inside and out and gave it to Katie. The gift was a mustard tin with pictures of cows standing in water painted on the side. Indeed, little rust marred its surface.

"It's beautiful, Thomas. Thank you."

His smile was large and definitely his own—an image that would endure in her mind.

A Handbill

On a warm Saturday in June, Conway sent Thomas off on a Band of Hope youth outing so he and Katie could have a little free time. As they walked to Hyde Park to listen to music, Conway said, "I don't care much for Band of Hope's religion, but should they keep Thomas on the straight and narrow, it'll be worth it. I'd rather he grow up to be like the rest of those prater bastards than become what my father was. They'll make him sign the pledge. It won't keep him from drinking, but he'll have to think about it."

Conway worried unnecessarily about Thomas drinking, but Katie would stay out of it. He was Conway's boy, as Annie was her girl. The couple had come to an unspoken agreement about that long ago.

They spent their afternoon near the bandstand, enjoying a sixteen piece brass band dressed in blue and gold uniforms and playing selections of American music. A pleasant change in the weather had brought cleaner air and all was fresh and new.

On one of the paved walks, Katie found a handbill for Dr. Carter Moffat's Ammoniaphone which was said to create artificial Italian air. With slogans like, *Recommended by the Best Physicians*, and, *Invaluable in all Pulmonary Affections*, it touted the Ammoniaphone as an aid to vocalists and public speakers. Since the greatest voices developed in Italy, it explained, it followed that Italian air was the key. Breath taken through the Ammoniaphone, a long tube charged with an aromatic chemical compound, *Resembles the soft, balmy air of the Italian Peninsula*. What really caught her attention was, *Has proved of the utmost value in the treatment of coughs*.

The Ammoniaphone was not the sort of thing that could be afforded right now, but one day in the future perhaps. The device could help with both breathing and singing. Katie folded the handbill and slipped it into a pocket.

On the way home, they passed through Covent Garden Market to see the flowers, fresh fruits, and vegetables. Perhaps Conway would get a taste for something interesting and he'd pay the price to buy it for their supper.

Annie was supposed to be off all day with friends, but Katie knew she was seeing Mr. Phillips. As many young couples courted in Covent Garden Market because of the beautiful colors and fresh smells, it wasn't a surprise to see Annie strolling along the avenue, arm in arm with her beau, carrying a tussie-mussie of white primrose. In the language of flowers it meant, *I can't live without you.*

Conway turned in their direction, and Katie's heart skipped a beat. The young couple had paused beside the fountain on the eastern side of the avenue. Katie gripped his shoulder and turned him around to face her. He looked at her with a frown. She produced a calm, sweet smile and then planted a kiss on his lips. "Thank you for a wonderful day out."

"You haven't kissed me in so long I'd forgotten what it felt like." A slight frown settled on his face. Finally he said, "You're quite welcome."

He turned back to continue southeast across the avenue, perhaps attracted by the fountain which sparkled brightly in the sunlight, but it wasn't exactly the direction they needed to take to get home, and he was headed straight toward the loving couple.

Katie took him by the arm and turned him again, then gestured as casually as she could toward the vendors at the southern side of the avenue. "If we can afford anything at all here," she said, "it will be found at these carts."

"I am not buying vegetables today," he said, turning again toward the fountain and couple. "We have potatoes at home."

"Yes, but I fancy a treat, don't you?" She put her arm around him in a loving, companionable way, as she turned them as one toward the wagons on the western side of the market.

Conway pulled himself free and stopped. He stared hard at Katie, his head cocked to one side. "What are you trying to keep me from, woman?"

Shock and innocence would be the best defense, but she wasn't pulling it off. "I—I were—"she began, but Conway cut her off."

"Be still," he said, and she became silent, her heart racing while he looked all around.

"I'm merely suggesting we deserve something special to end a wonderful day," she said too loudly, as his eyes turned in the direction of the loving couple.

Conway spotted them. He turned back to Katie. "You and your daughter have been keeping a secret, haven't you? Thomas said as much, but I didn't believe him."

"I don't know what you mean." Her words weren't believable.

"We'll see about that." He walked swiftly toward Annie and Mr. Phillips.

Katie hurried after him. She grabbed Conway again, jerking him to a halt, and he allowed it. Dropping all pretense, she said, "Please don't. You're not dressed well. Mr. Phillips will think less of Annie should he see you dressed as you are."

"My clothes are fine. This Mr. Phillips shall not think less of me for the holes you've patched. If he does, he's not for Annie."

The couple could be seen out of the corner of her eye. Perhaps they would become lost in the crowd as she spoke. "He's a man with a good income. He's become devoted to her."

Conway stared at her again, hard, as if he could penetrate her mind and see what else she might be hiding. "Yet you've tried to keep this from me."

People flowed around them, occasionally obscuring Annie and her suitor. "Because you want her to take my place and work with you," Katie said. "I want her to have a better life, and Mr. Phillips could make that possible."

"She's too young for you to be making her wedding plans. I am her father and I shall have a word with him. Remain here."

Conway located the couple in the crowd and caught up with them. Annie was plainly startled and distressed to see him, but she made introductions. Conway gestured toward Katie and Annie came to join her while the men spoke privately.

"He's spoiling everything," Annie said bitterly.

"He is your father. We couldn't keep it from him forever."

"Still, I'll be lucky if Mr. Phillips will even look at me after this."

"Don't get so high and mighty that you forget all your father has done for you." Katie had become so accustomed to defending Annie against Conway, she felt strange defending *him*, even though that was the right thing to do.

Annie bowed her head and remained silent.

Presently, Conway left Mr. Phillips and came to stand next to Katie. He turned to Annie with a stern expression and said, "Go to your beau. He'll escort you home."

Annie did as he said, and Katie and Conway left the market.

"Annie's Mr. Phillips smells of creosote," Conway said, wrinkling up his nose."

His family runs a lampblack factory."

"So he said." Conway became silent for a time as they walked, clearly lost in thought.

He's looking for an excuse to put a stop to Annie's courtship.

Finally he turned to her. "The execution of your cousin comes next week. I'm almost finished with his ballad. I must prepare to travel to Stafford."

Six months earlier, Katie's cousin, Charles Robinson, had been arrested for the murder of a woman, his lover, some said. He was a troubled man, prone to anger and violence, but that was not the way he'd always been. For a time, when they were both young, he had been sweet to Katie, and their interest in each other had led to her first kiss. She'd never forgotten it. The news of his conviction and impending execution was heartbreaking.

"I'll need Annie to help sell chapbooks at the hanging," Conway said. "She's too young to become serious about a man."

Seeing Charles hang would be horrible, but allowing her daughter to go to the execution was worse. "Annie is done with selling chapbooks," she said. "That's my job."

"You told me you once loved Mr. Robinson," Conway said. "How can you want to be at his hanging?" He shook his head emphatically. "No, you aren't the pretty girl you were. I need Annie's sweet face to draw attention."

"Yes, I loved him once. I still have a place for him in my heart. Should it be up to me, I would not have us earn money from his misery. He's part of my family."

"We can't afford to pass up the opportunity," Conway said.

"I don't want to see him hang, but I don't want Annie in danger. And you know she *cannot* sing."

"Dangers are everywhere," Conway said. He shook his head again. "You've lost the desire to attract a crowd. Your singing lacks the life it once had."

It's not the type of crowd I want to sing for. "Only because I don't enjoy the work," she said. "I *shall* do better. Give me another chance and allow Annie to be a child just a little longer."

"She's grown now and has had her time to be a child. I need her. She'll not marry until she's twenty-one years old."

He was too pragmatic and arguing with him never helped. Still, there must be a way to appeal to a part of him that was not strictly practical.

"Please allow her to stay behind this once," she said. "She is hardly healed from the last time."

Conway winced, and bowed his head.

That was it; he felt sorrow for her injury.

"The next cut might be to her pretty face," Katie said.

Gazing at his feet, he remained silent for a long while, then he looked Katie in the eye. "I suppose we can get along without her one last time."

A Silk and Velvet Dress Bodice and a Black Straw Bonnet

"We'll travel to your cousin's execution by rail," Conway said ,while Katie cleaned up the table after an evening meal. He held out third class tickets he'd purchased. "The fare wars between the lines have made travel by rail the best price." Traveling city to city in the crude wagons Conway hired had always been a trial. Going to Stafford in a London Northwest Railway carriage was going to be a treat, but being in a black mood over her poor cousin's eminent death, Katie turned away from Conway without a word and finished up her work.

They set out early for St. Pancras Station the morning of the execution and were in their railcar by 6:00AM. Her first time traveling by train, the vibration and unusual sounds became frightening. Yet as the train left London and picked up speed, the experience grew as intoxicating as the liquor she'd had many years earlier. Speeding downhill, over a river on a viaduct and into a valley, the dire reality of their visit to Stafford lost its power over her. Katie knelt on the hard wooden bench and leaned out of the small window behind it. She spread her arms like wings and yelled over the rushing wind, "We're flying!"

"We're going too fast," Conway said, pulling her back in. "The wind could break your neck." Clearly, he had become embarrassed. Though he insisted she take her seat, he smiled, making it easier to tolerate his demand.

Still breathless when they arrived at Stafford Station, Katie disembarked, giggling and holding Conway's hand. The purpose of the visit and a sense of sober reality returned to her as they walked to the prison with their bundles of chapbooks.

Charles Robinson was the son of her mother's sister, Martha. Aunt Martha and her family lived in Birmingham. On the few occasions when the families met, Charles paid close attention to Katie. The last time they met, six months before Catherine died, Martha had come to London for some purpose or another. She'd brought Charles and they stayed at an inn. Katie and Catherine went to visit them in their room and later they all had a delicious fish dinner at a local tavern. Martha paid for the meal. In the room and at the tavern, Charles sat close to Katie and tried to draw her out with conversation. She didn't make it easy for him. His constant and insistent eye contact unnerved, as well as excited, her. On the walk back to the inn from the tavern, the two mothers had become distracted by their own conversation.

"May I have a kiss?" Charles asked.

Katie shook her head, grinned, and turned away. To kiss him would be wonderful, but somehow the idea frightened her.

What a foolish little girl I am. I don't want to lose his attentions. If he asks me again, I'll kiss him passionately.

That left her wondering what passion felt like.

When they arrived at the inn, the adults went inside while Katie and Charles remained on the street out front. She leaned against the wall of the building while he stood close and talked about his life in Birmingham. What he had to say wasn't interesting, but he was handsome. After a while he became quiet and merely looked at her with a smile. Finally he put a finger under her chin, gently raised her face to meet his own, and kissed her lightly on the lips. A pleasant shiver ran through her, and for a moment she was in love.

"You two stop that right now," Aunt Martha's voice boomed from the front step of the inn.

Katie shied away from Charles. The shame came so swiftly, she grew dizzy.

Charles released her and headed for the door leading inside. Martha struck him on the crown of his head as he passed by.

Katie remained on the street until Catherine came to fetch her.

"He is your cousin," she said. "One day you'll find a proper love."

That moment of innocent desire had been held dearly in her heart ever since.

~ ~ ~

At the prison gate, as the hour approached for Mr. Robinson's execution, the crowd grew from perhaps one hundred to nearly a thousand. Through the afternoon Katie called on her charmed memories of the young Charles over and over as she sang the ballad lamentation contained in the chapbook. "The Awful Execution of Charles Colin Robinson" was sung to the tune of "Long Lost Ellen" by Noel Wincott.

Come all you feeling Christians,
Give ear unto my tale,
It's for a cruel murder
I was hung at Stafford Gaol.
The horrid crime that I have done
Is shocking for to hear,
I murdered one I once did love,
Harriet Segart dear.

Charles Colin Robinson is my name,
With sorrow was oppressed,
The very thought of what I'd done
Deprived me of my rest
Within the walls of Stafford Gaol,
In bitter grief did cry,
And every moment seemed to say
"Poor soul, prepare to die!"

I well deserve my wretched fate,
No one can pity me,
To think that I in my cold blood,
Could take her life away,
She no harm to me had done,
How could I serve her so?
No one my feelings now can tell,
My heart was so full of woe.

O while within my dungeon dark,
Sad thoughts came on apace,
The cruel deed that I had done
Appeared before my face,
While lying in my prison cell

Those horrid visions rise,
The gentle form of her I killed
Appeared before my eyes.

O Satan, thou demon strong,
Why didst thou on me bind?
O why did I allow thy chains
To enwrap my feeble mind?
Before my eyes she did appear
All others to excel,
And it was through jealousy
I poor Harriet Segart killed.

May my end a warning be
Unto all mankind,
Think on my unhappy fate
And bear me in your mind.
Whether you be rich or poor
Your friends and sweethearts love,
And God will crown your fleeting days,
With blessings from above.

At first, only a few gathered around the couple, but then Katie lifted her voice to express sorrow for her cousin's fate. She'd not expressed such feeling in song for a long time, and it felt good. With no hanging to watch, Katie's singing became the main attraction at the prison gate. The crowd grew quickly, and soon she and Conway were ringed in and surrounded. People in the rear pressed forward to get a better position while those in front defended their ground stoically, listening to Katie sing the ballad over and over before allowing others to take their place.

Conway took care of sales and business was brisk.

At one point, it became clear that word had been passed from the prison gate and a roar went up from the crowd. Katie knew that Charles Robinson was no more. She sang the song two more times as the crowd began to disperse. Throat sore and heart aching,

Katie was spent.

Conway, simply giddy, said, "We sold over four hundred copies!" He nearly shouted the words, breaking his own rule against talking about their earnings in public. "We had no right to expect as much from that small crowd, but your singing brought them in."

In the midst of a coughing spell, Katie didn't respond.

They stayed in an inn near the train station that night. Although Conway wanted to stay up talking, Katie had become exhausted. He was considerate enough to allow her to get some sleep. They caught an early train back to London the next morning, arriving mid-afternoon at St. Pancras Station.

Leaving the station, Conway took Katie by the arm and led her away from their intended route. "Where are you taking me?" she asked.

"There is a gift I'd like to offer you," he said, sweeping her down a side street. Katie smiled uncertainly while trying to keep up.

"You've wanted fine clothes for some time." He opened the door to a little shop below street level and they passed within. "If you'll always sing as you did in Stafford, we can't help but prosper. We can still further improve our lot by making you more attractive."

With Conway obviously so impressed with her singing, she easily tolerated his slight about her appearance.

"May I help you?" asked the shopkeeper, a round ginger-haired woman with pink cheeks and green eyes.

Katie was fitted for the green silk and black velvet bodice and skirt she'd always imagined she should have. To go with it, she chose a black straw bonnet trimmed with green and black velvet and black beads. She chose abalone buttons that had come all the way from Australia. All the fabrics were crisp and clean, and the buttons sparkled with newness under the numerous gas lamps that lit the interior of the shop. Conway paid the woman all he and Katie had earned the previous day and then some. He was told all would be ready in a week.

Katie felt so light, she hardly noticed the long walk home. Conway talked about plans for her singing at future executions, his smile flashing, eye winking, all that he said and did meant to inspire a sense of camaraderie and clever conspiracy.

She too had begun taking her singing seriously again, but her plans did not dovetail with his.

Arriving home, they were met at the door by a gloriously beaming Annie. "Mr. Phillips has proposed marriage!" she cried.

Conway didn't stand in the way of the marriage of Annie and Mr. Phillips.

"She is a treasure, but I shan't miss having to keep her in tuck and dunnage," he said.

"She's thin as a rail," Katie complained, "and I'm the one kept her clothed with cast-offs from the laundry."

Conway ignored her her grumbling. "Now that I have my Katie back, we'll do just fine." He referred to her singing.

Sensitive to the financial state of the bride's parents, Mr. Phillips suggested a small affair. Conspicuously, Conway made no effort to pay for anything. Clearly to save embarrassment on all sides, Mr. Phillips took care of the bills.

The wedding took place in a small brick church in Holborn. The happy day suffered the sad news that Charlotte Neet, who had been invited to the wedding, died in her sleep two nights before.

Mr. Phillip's father and two sisters were in attendance at the church, as well as Katie, Conway, Thomas, and Katie's sisters. She had located her sisters in Bermondsey by finding Emma's husband, Mr. Matthews, at the pub where he organized his lumpers. She'd had a tearful reunion with her sisters that included an apology to Emma for the way she'd spoken to her in the fish market years earlier.

After the wedding, Mr Phillips gave Katie the gift of a fine white cotton pocket handkerchief with red and white birds-eye border. Then he took Conway aside and said, "I'll take good care of Anne, but I want you to know, I'm not an easy mark for mumpers."

Conway looked under his beetling brow at his son-in-law and balled his fists. But after a moment he relaxed, swallowed his pride, and smiled, pretending he hadn't been called a beggar.

Annie is my second chance and she's leaving. But am I not going with her? Like a master ship builder, Katie had poured heart and soul into the creation of a beautiful vessel, only to see her launched under the command of an unknown captain piloting her into foreign, perhaps dangerous, waters. *The better part of me is going with her, while my thoughts remain behind, imprisoned in a derelict hulk.*

Katie had worn her new silk and velvet bodice, skirt and bonnet to the wedding, but in the weeks that followed she didn't have an opportunity grand enough to warrant wearing them again. Feeling hollow without Annie in her life every day, she needed a new goal to rise to each morning. Katie put the new clothes on for inspiration and the answer came to her in an instant.

~ ~ ~

The next morning, Katie sat on the bed, darning socks while Conway sat at the table reading. "Now as Annie is gone," she said, "and Thomas will start his apprenticeship with your printer, there's no reason why I should not add to our earnings as a singer."

Conway gave no response.

"The first thing would be for me to join the sing-alongs at the Adam and Eve," she said.

"There's too much drinking that goes on there," Conway said flatly, without looking up from his reading. "The temptation is too great—you'll take it up."

Clearly he intended that to mean *no* and for that to be the end of it, but Katie wasn't finished. "You could go with me."

Conway shook his head vigorously.

"I'd do it after supper and you could watch me." A pleading in her voice said she'd already lost the argument.

"I have no cause to want to do that," Conway said.

"You've never known me to take a drink, and have no reason to fear it now. Think of the money. Should I impress the landlord at the Adam and Eve, he might hire me to sing in The Garden of Eden—"

"Garden of Eden, ha!" Conway said with contempt. "That back room has grown to swallow most of the tavern proper. It is a den for drunkenness and debauchery. I can't eat my supper there without some lushington stumbling past my table with his dollymop. You start singing there, it'd soon be you hanging on his arm."

"You have no cause to talk to me like that." The outrage was worth a try. "You compare me to a *prostitute?*"

"Katie, dear, it's part of the job in those back rooms."

"That's *not* true." Letting the outrage go, she tried calm and reasonable. "There are perfectly respectable women who have performed there and gone on to find great fame. The impresarios of the great music halls—"

"How do you think they get hired?" Conway had returned to his matter-of-fact-tone. "You've heard what passes for singing in the music halls."

"I only know what I hear—"

"—And you've heard music hall singing. I sold my publican gin for those tickets two years ago to take you to Charring Cross Theatre."

"Yes, I remember. The singing was not good, but that only encourages me. I am so much better."

"*No.* We'll not talk about it again."

"We *will* talk about it." Katie said, her voice becoming shrill. "You have no reason not to trust me."

"*Don't* I?" Conway finally looked up. His aging face was heavily lined and bore stern features. "You took a bottle of gin from me long ago, and then, one day years later, returned it. I don't think you drank any of it, but you must have wanted it. One day you may want it again. You also kept money from me."

Katie's heart racing, her gaze narrowed as she looked to her memories. "How?"

"You think I'm such a glock, I shouldn't notice a loose board?"

Katie's scalp prickled, her jaw became tight, the grip she had on the sock and darning needle became painful. "Why wouldn't you say anything?"

"Why should I?" He said it too calmly. "If you'd done worse, I'd have put you out, but you didn't."

Her jaw popped under the pressure, sending pain along her teeth. The dull gray sock she held was turning red—she had punctured her left thumb with the fat, dull darning needle. "You are a cold man, Mr. Conway," she said, wide-eyed and raging. "You have played me for a fool. I wish I'd never met you!"

"By tomorrow you'll have changed your mind. From the day

we met, you've always known which side your bread is buttered on."

Her efforts as a young woman to seduce him to gain a new life undermined her righteous indignation. Her mother's words came back to her from long ago: "Life is hard on pretty girls. Pretty girls want things and have ways of getting them. Be careful what you do, Katie, to get what you want."

She turned her eyes away from Conway and he turned his back on her. She held her bleeding thumb as he moved to the door. No quicksilver welled up, nothing *good and pure*, only the ghastly red.

"I have business," he said without looking back. "I'll be back just before supper. We'll eat at the Adam and Eve, but there will be no singing."

"I *shall* sing for the landlord of the Adam and Eve, and he'll hire me for his back room!"

"I give you a choice, then, between me and the singing," Conway said, still facing the door. "If you choose to sing in those places, don't come back here. I shan't have you." He walked out and shut the door behind him.

Katie collapsed on the bed, her tears and blood dampening the bedclothes.

A Pair of Men's Lace Up Boots

I have little what isn't truly Conway's. He even keeps my secrets.

Since shortly after she'd come to live with Conway, Katie had confined her possessions to the two shelves he had given her in the set of five against the East wall of their room. Presently she had little more than when she arrived. The travel bag that had belonged to her mother had rotted away long ago, but it was an easy matter for her to gather up everything she owned and fold it all into a blanket to carry with her.

Katie would take with her what she'd given to their marriage. She found Conway's old waistcoat, the one she'd repaired on the day they met, and added it to her possessions in the blanket. The garment fit Katie better than it did Conway. Having repaired it with so many stitches over the years, it belonged to her now. With that as a new standard, she turned to a pair of Conway's boots she'd repaired with red thread. They were a little big for her, but those were added to her possessions out of spite.

She'd prefer to go to Annie and Mr. Phillips, but didn't want to embarrass her daughter by taking her troubles with Conway to her doorstep. No, she would go to Emma in Bermondsey.

Katie put on her fine silk and velvet bodice, skirt and bonnet. She looked around the room. Would she miss it? She remembered thinking of herself as fortunate when Charlotte praised her home, but that was when she'd believed Conway cared about her happiness.

I'll miss it only if Emma won't take me in and I have to sleep rough.

Katie left the room and walked southwest, coughing in the thick hazy air. She'd hardly made it to the nearest street crossing when Conway, coming from the right, saw her.

"Where are you going, dressed to the nines?" he asked.

Katie kept walking.

Approaching swiftly, he followed her across the street, got ahead and stopped, facing her. Katie pushed past, to continuing without a word. Conway reached for her, but she shrugged him off. He grabbed her upper arm and spun her around, ripping the shoulder of her bodice and popping loose the top two abalone buttons. They fell to the pavement. Conway's right foot trod on one. The other was kicked away into the street by her own clumsy efforts to maintain her footing. As she faced him, he stepped back a little, revealing the button under his foot. The bright piece of shell was broken in two.

"I asked where you're going."

Katie looked him in the eye. "I'm going for a visit with Emma."

"And why are you carrying a stuffed blanket?"

"My things," she said without emotion. "You gave me a choice. Should I stay with her and decide to sing, I won't be back."

"You have obligations to me."

"You *gave* me a choice."

Conway stared at her for a moment.

Her gaze remained level and calm.

A troubled look gripped his features and he aged in that moment, before her eyes. Ten years her senior, perhaps he hadn't expected to be alone and didn't want that future. For a moment his expression said he regretted the way he'd treated her, but clearly his pride would never allow him to admit it. Nor would it allow him to keep her from leaving after giving her the choice.

"Don't stay long," he said.

Katie stepped around him and walked away.

"We have work to do," he called after her. "You have responsibilities."

She didn't look back.

Three Abalone Buttons

Katie had easily impressed the landlord of The Black Anchor, Fredrick Poulton, with her singing. He hired her to sing in his back room for a wage based on how much drink was sold during the hours of her performance. His math was intentionally complicated. Katie would be cheated, but she had her chance and that was what mattered.

Mr. Poulton gave her songs to learn that celebrated drinking as a salvation for the working man, that ridiculed marriage and condemned labor as slavery. The songs were poorly written and the music lacked character.

The Black Anchor's back room was named The Four Winds, and it did seem a likely spot for farts to convene. The area was twenty by forty feet, its walls painted with a thin coat of bright red paint. The sagging floor supported twenty rough, round tables and too many rickety chairs. When singing, she occupied a clearing in one corner.

In the two months she'd been at it, she'd received much praise for her performances. She'd also been ogled, laughed at, pawed, and even spat upon. Katie put all she had into her voice and endured the abuse. One night someone from one of the great music halls would come in and hear her and be inspired to hire her for the stage.

Her fine silk and velvet clothes looked older by the day and were a fair reflection of the way Katie felt. She had repaired the ripped shoulder of the bodice. Emma had given her five brass buttons to replace the five abalone ones. Katie saved the three abalone buttons that remained until such time she might replace the two that were lost and put them all back on the bodice. The garment didn't look as good with brass, but it would do for now.

The Black Anchor stood not a mile of Emma's home in Bermondsey; an easy walk in the early evening, but a somewhat frightening one when she was returning home late at night. She got in the habit of walking most of the way with one of the barmaids, Rebecca Fitwerks, who lived near Emma. The two women had in common the fact that they had both left their husbands. They enjoyed having a smoke together and sharing their experiences on their walks home.

"It's good to be away from Richard," Rebecca said one night about her husband, "but I don't truly have a home now. Barbara has a new beau. She's asked me to find other lodgings."

"Barbara Olesen," Katie asked, "the barmaid?"

"Yes."

"I too have no real place to call my own," Katie said. "I fear at any time I might be asked to leave my sister's home. Emma received me with open arms, but Mr. Matthews told me he wouldn't go against another man's will when it came to his wife. Should Conway come for me, he said, he'd have to turn me out. I give Mr. Matthews most of my earnings and do what I can to help. We get along well, but he complains about the crowding, and I know he's looking for a reason to put me out. Perhaps he thinks if he does I'll return to Conway. I would go to my daughter before I would return to him."

Katie had sent Annie a letter, telling her she was staying with Emma, and was troubled she hadn't hear back from her.

"It is the way with men," Rebecca said. "A good man will stand with a cruel one when it comes to his wife. The neighbors could see my bruises, but none would help me. Men want us in the worst way, but they don't trust us. I shall not return to Richard. I won't live that way again."

Rebecca stopped walking and turned to Katie with bright eyes. "We could get lodgings together," she said.

Katie smiled hesitantly. Others at The Black Anchor had said Rebecca periodically turned to prostitution to get by. The idea of Rebecca bringing strange men into her home was unsettling. Katie shrugged as they continued walking. "I know Mr. Matthews isn't happy with me being there," she said, "but I pay so very little. A bit more and he'd be happy enough."

"You said it's crowded."

"Yes, there's also my other sister, Margaret and Mr. Matthews's youngest brother and his wife and two young boys. Margaret is quiet, too quiet. Something inside her were broken in the workhouse long ago. The little boys are a terror. Emma is glad to have me, but perhaps only because she gets so cold in the night. Mr. Matthews sleeps in another room because of his loud snoring and I sleep with Emma. She cuddles up close. I don't mind. It's nice and warm."

Rebecca didn't seem disappointed. "Let me know if things change," she said.

~ ~ ~

Mr. Matthew's grumbling increased. When Monday came, a day when Katie didn't sing at The Black Anchor, she took the time to go see Annie and ask for money.

Surely Mr. Phillips would not begrudge her a little help if she did it only once. Conway was the one he considered a beggar, not Katie.

She spent much of the morning walking the three and a half miles to her daughter's home, a modest little house in Holborn. The dwelling belonged to Mr. Phillip's family and was of the old type of architecture almost gone from London, with its heavy wooden beams and projecting upper story. She stepped up and knocked on the door and waited. She'd begun to think no one was home, then heard movement inside and the door opened.

"Mum!" Annie said. "Come in." She'd hastily dressed and looked slightly bent.

"I'm sorry for the surprise. Did I wake you?"

"No, I've been ill, but I'm getting better."

"What is it? Why didn't you call on me to help?"

"Some say it's the water again," she said, embracing her abdomen. "Many people hereabouts have it. I didn't want to bother you. It's almost over now."

Katie cupped Annie's cheeks in her hands. "My sweet girl," she said.

Annie's lips tightened into a forced smile. "Why have you come?" she asked.

She doesn't want to be treated like a child. She is my better now.

Katie released her and stepped back. She swallowed hard and lowered her gaze. "You received my letter?"

"Yes."

Why then hasn't she written to me?

Because she's been ill.

"Then you know I have left your father and am staying with your Aunt Emma and her family. I am singing at a tavern, The Black Anchor, in their back room, The Four Winds."

"That's wonderful. You have such a beautiful voice."

"Yes, but Mr. Matthews will not continue to have me should I fail to give more to the family budget."

"And so you shall return to Papa?"

Will she make me beg?

"No. I'd hoped you might help."

Annie became silent for a moment. Then, as if it had suddenly dawned on her what her mother was asking for, she had a look of concern. "I would if I could, but you know Mr. Phillips will not wish to help. At present, I have two shillings I can give you, but he'll know about it and won't be pleased."

I came all this way for something as makes no difference.

Clearly Annie saw the disappointment on her face.

How embarrassing.

Annie turned to a small cabinet by the door, opened a drawer, and took out two coins. "If it will help, please take it." She offered them to Katie.

"I earn that much in a day," The pride in her voice was too much.

"It's all I have." Annie's eyes held a look of hurt.

What has left her feeling wounded? I'm the one who has need!

"I'm sorry I troubled you while you're ill." Chagrin that she couldn't keep the indignation out of her voice turned to more anger. "I'll come back for a visit when I am richer, when I have work in a music hall." She turned away to start the long walk home.

"Mum, I'm sorry," Annie said. "I would give more if I had it."

She continued to plead for her mother to be reasonable, to come back and start their visit anew. Annie's voice receded into the distance as Katie walked swiftly toward the river and the Waterloo Bridge that would take her home. She felt fortunate that in recent years the bridge had been nationalized, the toll for foot traffic no longer required.

How can it be that Parliament is looking out for me more than my own flesh and blood? That was foolishness—her anger had got the better of her again.

The last thing she heard from Annie was, "You can always go home to Papa."

To rest up a bit before beginning the return trip would have been good. She wasn't used to so much exercise. Coughing fits dogged her all the way home.

Since Katie had endured Conway's close scrutiny when it came to finances, she well understood her daughter's situation with Mr. Phillips. That evening she sent a letter of apology to Annie.

Tuesday night after work Katie and Rebecca walked home together.

"I don't know what I'll do, should Mr. Matthews put me out."

"You know there are men willing to pay for companionship," Rebecca said.

Katie shook her head and turned away, but Rebecca was undeterred. "Men of all sorts, gentle ones among them. If you need to know who they are to safely earn a bit extra, ask any of us girls working The Black Anchor."

Katie's reaction wasn't one of moral superiority and she didn't want her words to be received as such. She looked Rebecca in eye and said. "Thank you. I'm just afraid. I've never done that."

But haven't I, with Uncle William.

"Most of the men are so drunk," Rebecca said, "they don't know or care if they're getting it right. A little firkytoodle is all it takes for some."

Katie turned away again, blushing.

"For others," Rebecca continued, "one moist hole is as good as another."

Katie had tricked Uncle William. If she could do it that way, it wouldn't be so bad.

"Think about it," Rebecca said. "There *are* some decent ones. I couldn't get along without the help."

Yes, I could try. It's worth it to remain here and sing. I'm not too proud for that.

~ ~ ~

Katie's experience was much like what Rebecca had suggested and her own plan worked—a little saliva spread on the insides of her legs, and her technique of squeezing her upper thighs tightly around a man's penis worked flawlessly. The plan worked until the night she made the mistake of choosing the man herself.

He had been making eye contact with her much of the night while she sang. Perhaps forty years old, he had sandy blonde hair and a round, handsome face despite a crooked nose. His fine clothing made him stand out among the laborers who were The Black Anchor's main clientele. The way he looked at her, the gentle longing in his eyes, suggested he was like the other ones.

A storage room for barrels of wine and spirits was used by some of the women for their transactions. Once Katie had taken the man into the room and shut the door, he changed. His face became cold and angry. She wanted out, but he stood between her and the door. Katie took in a deep breath to cry out for help, but he struck her in the face so hard she blacked out momentarily. When she came to, she was draped, face down, over a barrel and he was brutally penetrating her anus.

"No!" she screamed, jerking herself up and back. She had to fight. The table knife was in its pocket under her skirt, if she could get to it.

He struck her in the back of the head and she fell forward, dazed.

"Sing for me!" he shouted, plunging deeper inside her, but Katie cried out in pain. "Don't scream! Sing for me." His voice was deep and guttural. He struck her again, and as she swam back up to full consciousness again, something told her to try to become calm.

"Sing, damn it, sing!"

Katie tried to reach her right hand under her skirt to grab her knife, but he pulled that arm behind her back and up. Pain tore through the muscles of her arm and shoulder. She pushed all thoughts from her head and concentrated on what he wanted. Katie sang, haltingly at first, the piece she'd last sung, an inane song titled "Drinking Your Troubles Away."

He pulled out of her anus and penetrated her vagina, matching his thrust to the rhythm of the song. "Better—you must do better, louder!" he shouted.

Crushed against the barrel, her arm pulled up behind her, she had a difficult time filling her lungs and belting out the song, but she did her best, lifting her voice higher and fuller.

Then it was over. A draft was cooling her bare behind as his seed spilled out of her and ran down her legs. The door was open and he had fled. But the world beyond the door was too frightening, for *he* remained out there, somewhere.

Katie relaxed against the barrel, retreating from consciousness, until Barbara Olesen discovered her some time later and helped her to fix her skirts and regain her composure. As they were leaving the storeroom, Katie kicked an object with a shuffling step. Something red with white metal fittings slid into view on the floor.

The barmaid stooped to pick it up. "You dropped your cigarette case," she said.

Katie accepted it and put it in a pocket.

A Printed Calling Card

Katie didn't return to The Black Anchor for two weeks. Emma and family were sympathetic, but Katie was left to take care of herself during the day as everyone in the household had daytime responsibilities.

Rebecca came to see her, but didn't stay long. She said that no one at the tavern remembered seeing the man.

Perhaps it didn't really happen.

The aches and pains would not allow the denial for long. Lumps and bruises on her head were the least of her troubles. Two days after the rape, Katie began to feel an incessant need to urinate, but had difficulty doing so. When she succeeded, there was an intense burning sensation and the flow contained blood. As the week progressed, she spent many hours in bed, and increasingly more time with the chamber pot or in the privy out back. To distract herself from the pain as she squatted or sat, struggling for relief, she'd press the second finger of her right hand into her thimble until it hurt.

Angrily, she plucked at her regret, shame, resentment, and self pity, trying to tease out the loose ends and unravel the tangle of her thoughts. But the more she plucked, the more the tangle rolled around, presenting the same thoughts and feelings over and over and exposing her rage.

She revised her memory of the rape to allow her to pull her sharp table knife from its pocket and slam it into the rapist's face over and over. But that was merely a fantasy. He had got away with it. Nothing could change that.

Then the anger turned.

I chose him! Foolish. Poor judge of character. Too daft to leave it in the hands of the barmaids. Shouldn't be on my own.

Her voice had somehow provoked him to rape her. Perhaps because she drew attention publicly, she had brought it all upon herself.

Everyone at The Black Anchor knew what happened even if no one saw the man. Along with the shame of that, a dread gripped her that she would never sing again without thinking of what happened, thinking about *him.*

I cannot go back. If I return to sing at The Four Winds, it shall happen again.

Wasn't Conway warning me about this? Life with him were good most of the time. He was cold-hearted, but still a decent man. He would take me back. I could go home. I must try.

The decision was firm, if unsatisfactory, until suddenly it was not.

Foolish thoughts! My singing is nothing but a pleasure. No one need suffer for it.

The criminal not only took her sexually, he violated her singing as well.

I could not have known. His kindly face was part of a deception. He were hunting and I fell into his trap, nothing more.

Should I allow his violation to take this from me, I make his cruel act whole and complete. I can't do that.

The decision was made mid-afternoon, leaving enough time for her to get ready to go to work. Katie prepared quickly, dressing and eating a small meal. She drank little liquid with it to prevent the intense need to relieve herself on the walk to The Black Anchor.

Emma came home just as Katie left. "I saw your Conway at market today. He said he was looking for you, wants you to come home. Should he have you back, perhaps it's time."

Katie shook her head. She had almost succeeded in bargaining with herself a return to her old life, but she still had her singing. No good reason existed for Conway to be strolling through the markets where her sister bought her goods. Had Mr. Matthews sent Emma looking for him? None of it mattered.

"I have to get to work or I'll be late," she said and hurried on.

Katie immediately used one of the outhouse privies in the back before entering The Black Anchor. Inside, Mr. Poulton saw her and approached. "If you'd stayed out longer, I'd've had to sack you," he said sternly.

Katie frowned and looked away.

"But I'm glad you're back," he said, squinting at her comically. "You were missed."

Katie smiled.

"I called on Victoria to take your place tonight, but she won't mind giving it up. She didn't want to come in anyway."

Katie thanked him and entered The Four Winds. As Mr. Poulton suggested, Victoria was happy to go home. Katie got a glass of water to place on the small table in the corner, took up her position and, when the time came for her to start, she was ready to sing.

The pressure her diaphragm placed on her bladder as she sang caused her voice to emerge with more force, slightly higher in pitch and with greater volume. Katie struggled to control her breathing to relieve the pressure and discovered new, more effective ways to modulate her voice. She carefully sipped water between songs, taking enough to moisten her throat against the bitter, smoke-charged air, but not so much that she added to the problem of having to frequently relieve herself. Even so, after every few songs Katie endured the disappointment of her audience as she took a break to visit the privy. She feared she'd lose the tavern its patrons, but upon her return each time she saw the same faces at the tables, along with new ones. They applauded her songs as never before. Head held high and her heart beating with renewed hope, she stepped away from her corner during a scheduled break.

Rebecca approached. "There's a man named Carver wanting to meet you and buy you a drink. He's in the tavern proper. He's a booking agent who has the ear of the promoters at Wilton's in Whitechapel. He got them to hire Ellen Byrn, Marie Courtenay, and Alice Hurley."

Katie froze as she listened to Rebecca, her flesh tingling with excitement. The names meant little, except for that of Alice Hurley, whose affair with a black man from Paris had given rise to increasingly scandalous stories in the press.

Such excitement over something as common as a dalliance! Could that happen to me?

Rebecca looked at her expectantly.

Katie had stopped breathing. She shook herself and gulped a breath. "Yes, take me to him," she said urgently.

She took deep, even, calming breaths as she followed Rebecca through the crowded tavern, weaving between the tables filled with jovial and raucous patrons toward the front of the establishment. She split her lip chewing on it and had to decide to leave it alone. Rebecca was not moving swiftly enough. Katie looked to the left and right, craned her neck to see beyond her guide's taller head and shoulders, trying to get her first look at the man. Finally Rebecca stopped, gestured toward a gentleman seated alone at a table by the front window, then walked away.

He faced the window, watching her reflection as she approached, his features reflected in the glass slowly coming into focus; sandy blonde hair, round cheeks and crooked nose. She froze not five feet away from him.

Did he watch me again tonight? Should I tell Mr. Poulton the criminal is here? Would I be believed since no one saw him?

"If you want to move from here to the music hall," he said, his deep voice calm and reasonable. "You'll have to talk to me."

Katie had been ready to bolt, but he'd caught her attention, and better, he'd cast a bright spark of hope into her imagination with only the one sentence. The world outside her experience, beyond her imagination, shifted suddenly, and she found herself moving with it and considering something unthinkable as she asked herself how much she wanted to sing in a music hall.

"Come and sit," he said. "I've bought you a whiskey." He stood and pulled out a chair for her. "My name is Frank Carver. I'm very much interested in your singing." He offered her a calling card, with his name and address printed on it.

He has no fear of being revealed.

Nothing but appearance suggested he was the man who had raped and beaten her. *It must be his twin brother.* No, the violent man was here. He could be that man in an instant.

Still, the spark he'd cast had lit a fire in her mind. Katie imagined the response she'd got from tonight's audience multiplied by twenty or more in a high-ceilinged hall with proper lights and musicians to support her voice.

She sat down.

"Wilton's in Whitechapel could use a voice like yours," Mr. Carver said.

Katie tried to look at him and smile, but could manage only a glance. Questions about the possibilities and the process of being hired by Wilton's occurred to her, but she couldn't find her voice.

Out of sight beneath the table top, Katie's hands felt around in her pockets—nothing but fidgeting perhaps, because of her agitated state.

How can he make pleasant conversation with me after what he did, as if none of it happened? Does he think what he's done is acceptable because of what he has to offer?

"You *are* interested in such a situation, *aren't* you?" Mr. Carver sounded impatient. He lit a cigar, and then a candle-lamp on the table which he slid over next to Katie. "Please look at me," he said.

Her right hand found the thimble in her pocket. Catherine would not approve of what she was doing, but she had given her the thimble for protection of a sort, and it had always brought Katie comfort. By reaching inside with a finger to touch the silver, she touched her mother.

She coughed several times, then took a deep, steadying breath and looked him in the eye. Despite the composed and handsome figure he cut, his features *were* anger and violence. In exchange for his help, she would endure his brutality again and again.

Even so, she managed to smile brightly for him. He smiled back around the glowing ember of his cigar, an expression meant to engender confidence. And it worked, for Katie finally found her voice. "I would be pleased to be considered by the promoters at Wilton's."

"We'll have to get you over there straight away." Mr. Carver placed his hand on her thigh and she flinched, but he had no reaction and left his hand there. "You have a great voice, and it must be getting better by the moment, for the first performance I attended was good, but nothing compared to what I heard tonight."

"Do you mean my performance in the store room?" Katie asked, an edge of accusation in her tone. She didn't know why she'd said that and immediately regretted it. Somehow her mouth had betrayed her. The question reminded her of the sort of sarcastic scorn Catherine used to give her when she knew Katie was dissembling.

Mr. Carver removed his hand from her thigh, took the cigar out of his mouth and leaned back, staring hard at her for a moment.

Katie stared back with equal intensity, her features set in a subtle expression of defiance. Her anger had got the better of her again, but it felt good and she couldn't help it. Still, she wanted to sing in a music hall, and this was her chance. Surely she could control herself long enough to win the prize.

"If you don't get work through me," Mr. Carver said coldly, "you'll never make it to the music halls. I'll see to that."

Katie swallowed hard, then looked him in the eye. "I'm sorry," she said, struggling against disgust and outrage. "I *do* want this."

Mr. Carver shifted the candle lamp from side to side, examining Katie's face. Awaiting his response, she froze, caught between conflicting desires.

"You gave me a cold look and it revealed your age," he said. "Too bad I didn't meet you ten years ago."

Nonplussed, Katie's mouth opened to speak the words that would turn the conversation back in a more favorable direction. But what might they be? None came to mind.

"The music halls need much younger talent. Now that I see you more clearly, I know mere makeup will not be enough."

No, it's only my voice that matters, her mind screamed, but they were not the right words and so could not find their way out.

"Oh," Mr. Carver said, as if a thought had suddenly occurred to him. "I dropped my cigarette case, perhaps in the store room. Did you happen to find it?"

Stunned by his callousness, Katie could only shake her head slowly, stupidly. Mr. Carver looked at her frozen features for a moment and chuckled.

"Too bad. It was a gift." He got up abruptly and walked out of The Black Anchor, leaving Katie sitting before the glass of whiskey he'd bought her. The haze of his cigar smoke remained, hanging over her like a pall.

I'm too old. I waited too long. All those wasted years waiting for Conway to change. He knew all along my hope would rape me.

And all the time spent defending Annie's childhood so her life would be better. And for what—two shillings when I need so much more? Her life is *better, whilst mine....* The bitterness toward Annie could not be helped, but it burned a hole in her heart.

Katie's head ached as she plucked uselessly at the threads of her regret and resentment, trying to loosen them. They were too tight, too deep, and tied off so neatly they would never come undone.

Katie couldn't face it, and the whiskey offered a way out, an escape craved for years. She would drink it and order another and then another until she was insensible, oblivious to the pain that gripped head and heart. Rebecca would see that she got home all right. Tomorrow she would take the long walk back to Conway. If he *did* want her, so much the better. If not, she'd beg him to take her back.

Katie wiped the tears from her eyes. Then she raised the glass of whiskey to her lips at the moment Conway entered the front door of the tavern, not ten feet away.

He saw her and stopped dead in his tracks, a smile beginning to frame his lips.

Yet it didn't spread.

Paralyzed with astonishment, Katie still held the drink to her mouth. The fumes stung her nose.

Conway's eyes narrowed as he took in the scene.

I haven't taken the drink! I'll tell him what happened.

But she didn't move. She *wanted* the whiskey.

Conway's expression told her he knew what she was drinking, and that it was too late.

No! I'll explain everything...and...

His mouth tightened in disgust.

...and...he'll never believe me!

Without a word, Conway turned on his heels and walked out of The Black Anchor.

The door to her old life had closed forever.

Fresh tears rolled down her cheeks and tumbled from her upper lip into the drink. Still, she didn't move, breathing in the fumes. The liquor's smell of death and decay suggested the swift passage of time and the healing of wounds.

Finally, she tipped her head back and swallowed her tears with the whiskey.

A Tooth Comb and a Large White Handkerchief

Since the night Conway turned his back on her at The Black Anchor, she'd been unable to live without alcohol to dull the sharp edges of life. After that first drink, the desire for more had not left her, and there was never enough. While she had known much hunger and privation in life, never had she experienced such nagging urgency to *earn the price of more*.

She had not gone back to The Black Anchor. Her drinking was the excuse Mr. Matthews needed to justify her expulsion from his home. Emma unhappily accepted his decision.

Her first drunken binge lasted nearly a month, during which she stayed in the casual ward of the Bermondsey workhouse. The task-mistress there, a hard woman, had Katie scrubbing cells day and night. The harsh labour and conditions wore her down until she had to make a change. She cleaned herself up and took the long walk to her daughter's home, carrying everything she owned with her, rolled into a blanket.

She knocked on the door, and as she waited, she thought of how best to present herself. She straightened her clothing and knocked the soil off her boots. Despite the back pain she suffered from the hard labor, she struggled to stand straight and tall. She tried out several types of smiles and finally abandoned them all. When the door open abruptly, she let out a startled cry.

"Mum, you look terrible," Annie said.

Katie knew it was the truth and she couldn't pretend otherwise. She broke down in tears and hugged Annie. "Please take me in." she said.

"Yes, of course, do come in." Annie led Katie into the house to a small parlor.

Once they were seated, Katie gathered herself together. "No," she said, "I mean *please take me in*. I've nowhere else to go. I have come from the workhouse."

Annie's face expressed horror and she said nothing for a time.

She's reacting to me the way I did to my sisters when they came from the workhouse. She won't want to have anything to do with me.

Annie's look of disbelief changed to one of understanding and sympathy. "Yes," she said finally.

Excitement sent Katie into a coughing fit, but she suppressed it to hear what her daughter had to say.

"Mr. Phillips shall accept it if you're here to take care of me. I never fully recovered from the illness I had when you were last here. There's much I still can't do around the house. Don't you worry. Let's get you settled."

Katie had dreamed long ago that in her declining years, Annie would embrace her and keep her, making her old age tolerable. A wave of relief washed over Katie and engulfed her. Then she was rising back up out of darkness.

Annie stood over her, fanning her with a newspaper. "Mum, are you all right?"

"Yes, I...I haven't eaten well for some time."

Annie fed her mother and prepared a bath for her. When Katie was finished, Annie settled her in an upstairs room with a bed, wash basin, a flannel, hand towel, and a tooth comb.

Mr. Phillips was clearly not pleased that evening when he got home and heard Annie's plan. Katie remained in her room, listening to their argument through the walls. With time, their raised voices quieted, as if an agreement had been reached. Katie didn't suffer the suspense long. Annie came up to see her.

"It's settled," she said. "You'll stay and attend to my needs."

Katie smiled and clutched Annie's hands. "Thank you." She shook and Annie held her.

When Katie had become calm, Annie leaned back and produced a tight smile. "Mr. Phillips is most concerned about drinking. We heard about what happened in Bermondsey."

"I will not—" Katie started, but Annie cut her off.

"I told him I'd never known you to take a drink, that the circumstances had been extraordinary, and that if you did it in the future, just as he does, it would be in moderation and for good health."

Katie nodded her head, but remained silent. She craved a drink, but had decided that she must give it up. With the new opportunity, the comfort of a fine home, a warm bed, and the love of family, that shouldn't be difficult.

~ ~ ~

Before the week was out, Katie had found a bottle of Mr. Phillip's sherry while she was getting the dishes out of a cabinet to serve dinner. She returned to the cabinet the next day while cleaning house.

Any reasonable person could take just one swallow to relax, she told herself firmly. *I'll have that and no more.*

In the afternoon of the next day, after sweeping out the downstairs, she came back to the bottle and had another, larger swallow. The warm feeling spreading out from her belly provided a deep feeling of wellbeing.

An hour later, Annie decided to lie down for a nap until Mr. Phillips arrived home at supper time. Katie went back for more sherry, and then still more. With each drink, she more easily justified the next.

Then she was being awakened by Mr. Phillips. "Where's Annie?"

Katie almost fell out of her chair. The bottle of sherry, nearly empty, slipped from her grasp, hit the floor, and rolled until it struck Mr. Phillip's shoe and stopped.

"I'm here," came Annie's sleepy voice from the stairs.

"There's no supper," he said, stooping to pick up the bottle.

At the bottom of the stairs, Annie paused, taking in the scene. "Oh, Mum," she said.

"Tomorrow," Mr. Phillips said, "your mother shall go home to Mr. Conway."

The dream has come and gone so quickly. Katie felt numb.

Then, as her drunken torpor fled, she faced fear of the street, the workhouse, and herself.

~ ~ ~

She didn't understand how it could have happened. She stood outside the front door of her daughter's house the next morning, saying goodbye.

Mr. Phillips had little to say and had gone back in. Annie kept talking about Conway, but Katie wasn't listening.

Why can't I drink only a little, like the countless people in the world who take just enough and no more? How had she failed to control herself when the dream of her declining years was at stake? She could hardly blame Mr. Phillips and Annie for their reaction. Still, it hurt, for Annie didn't stand up for her.

Shouldering her blanket full of possessions, Katie wept.

"I'm sorry, Mum," Annie said. "Please go home to Papa." She pressed a white handkerchief into her mother's hand as she sent her away. Walking toward the East, Katie began to cough. As she wiped her mouth and nose with the handkerchief, she discovered the coins that were hidden in its folds, a crown, and a florin.

~ ~ ~

The money allowed her to stay in a common lodging for a few days and buy food and drink. While there, Katie met a man named Jon Kelly. He was a sometime market porter and full time drunkard in need of a partner. And she was desperate. Katie knew she would never have tender feelings for him, but he was a decent sort and would provide her with some protection. She would need it if she was going to drink.

Two Small, Blue Bed Ticking Bags

In April of 1888, Katie was 46 years old. She had been with Jon Kelly six years. They lived together in common lodgings in London's East End when they could afford it, in the casual wards when times were tough. Because Katie had to keep everything she owned on her person while she slept to protect it, she sewed two bed ticking bags to add to all the pockets she wore under her skirts.

Her health suffered, but she sought no remedies. Katie had lost most of her back teeth and had to be careful what she ate. She had increasing occurrence of severe back pain in the area of her kidneys and had endured the excruciating pain of passing multiple stones with her urine. The condition of being unable to catch her breath came more frequently, but was at its worse on the numerous occasions when her tissues held onto fluid, making her whole body feel bloated and tight.

Katie earned money in a variety of ways, such as running errands or charring for shops and common lodgings, but these jobs could be found only when she was washed and carrying herself well, a set of conditions becoming increasingly rare. On the occasions her cough permitted, she sang on the streets as a busker. If begging, she wore an imploring look on her face, and a ticket pinned to her breast that told a sad tale. When all else failed, she took to prostitution.

Since the autumn of 1887 several single women, about Katie's age, had been stabbed to death and left on the streets in the East End. No doubt they were victims of the Gully Bleeders, a gang that took protection money from prostitutes. Mr. Kelly's presence in Katie's life had protected her from them so far. He wasn't good for much, but he had a way with a knife.

Katie frequently spent what little she earned on drink instead of food. She had been in the habit of selfishly consuming her food and drink before reuniting in the evenings with Mr. Kelly, but since the recent spate of murders, she shared everything she could with him. More than ever, Katie was afraid of being on her own, and did her best to keep Mr. Kelly's interest.

A piece of Blue and White Shirting, Three-Cornered

In early September, 1888, with a terrible ache in her head and cramps in her belly that could only be soothed by more drink, Katie stalked her daughter in Holborn, looking for an opportunity to ask for money. The pursuit had become a habit, something she did every month or two. Each time, Annie showed a little more disgust and contempt. When Annie was younger, Katie had been delighted by the idea that she knew her daughter's mind, shared her thoughts and experienced her emotional states. Now she tried to deny what she knew full well; Annie's thoughts and feelings were plain to see on her face. Katie was compelled to endure the shame of it out of hunger and thirst.

Lingering within sight of the front door to Annie's house, she peeked around the corner from the nearest street crossing two houses away. She endured cold looks from those of the neighborhood who passed by on the street. What they saw in Katie was unmistakably clear in their mute expressions; with her many layers of clothing, unkempt appearance and the odor of her unwashed body and clothing, she was the embodiment of weakness and failure, of arrogant, willful shamelessness, an insufferable wretch.

With more drink in her belly, she would not care what they thought. Although it didn't work as well as it once had, alcohol could be depended on as a buffer against all her woes; her aches and pains, her fear of each day and the coming night, her dread of the future, and her progressive infirmity.

When deep in her cups, she could be who she wanted to be, for it set her imagination free. She became a person who stayed with Jon Kelly because he was aging and a drunkard who needed help getting along in the world. She ate little and had no real home because she was past the time in life when the consistency of such things was necessary for raising a family. If she fell asleep in an alley between crates, it was because it was comfortable enough and the weather had permitted it, and had nothing to do with the fact that she had passed out while playing Grandmother's Trunk with the ghost of her dead mother.

Her imagination had worked over her past as well. One day, she decided she'd indeed touched Catherine through the silver inside her thimble that last night at The Black Anchor. Once that was the truth, it was an easy matter to blame her mother for thwarting her efforts to work for Frank Carver. Catherine had taken over her voice and facial features to express defiance.

She were protecting me from a terrible temptation.

During their occasional visits, Katie never brought it up with her mother because she didn't want to spoil their time together. Her mother disapproved of the life Katie led, but out of love, held her tongue. Several times lately, Catherine had cradled Katie's face in her hands and said, "Your suffering shall be over soon." She was afraid to ask her mother what she meant.

When Katie was not drunk, she didn't believe such fantasies were real. Catherine was dead and gone, her thimble merely a thimble. Her life was a deep and overflowing cesspit that could never be cleaned. With no hope, no love, Katie's only refuge was drink, and she would always return to it as quickly as she could.

Annie emerged from her house and walked east along the street toward Katie. When she was close Katie stepped up to the corner and smiled for her. Annie stopped and clearly struggled to smile. "Mum, I cannot help you this time."

At least she didn't tell me again how bad I look.

"But you always have a little something for me."

"I do, and then I suffer for it when Mr. Phillips finds out. I can't pretend it's good to see you."

How can she stand so close, in her clean blue and white cotton skirt and warm shawl, and deny my need?

"I *am* your *mother*," Katie said miserably.

Outrage hardened Annie's features. "Oh...but what you've *done* to my mother," she said almost too quietly to hear. Then she spoke up. "You've shattered my memories of the one who loved and cared for me, who sacrificed to protect me. Every month you come to give me a glimpse of hatred, madness, and death." Tears streamed down her cheeks. "You come to me from the bowels of the city," Annie cried, "smeared with filth...reeking of disease...to ask for money."

Katie could only stare in horror, knowing exactly how Annie

saw her, for a mirror had shown the same only recently. The memory was vague because she had been deep in her cups. Perhaps it had been a late afternoon—she couldn't quite recall—when her reflection appeared in a shard of a broken mirror propped up in an abandoned shop window as she passed by on the street. She stared at her image, unbelieving. Who was the impostor wearing the aspect of filth and madness her sisters had worn like a costume when they lived in the workhouse? She knew it was her own image, but it was not the way she saw herself. She shook her arms, expecting the costume to fall away in tatters. When it did not, she panicked and flailed her arms and legs. She screamed and turned away from the mirror and fled.

Yes, there is a madness about me. I'm not just wearing it. I'm not playing a role. I am a filthy, drunken, muck-snipe whore.

Annie had fixed her gaze on the pavement at her feet. "You frighten me," she said pitifully. "What vermin do you bring to my doorstep? What illness might you leave with me?"

Katie touched the piece of blue and white shirting on her head. She'd picked it up at the common lodging that morning to bind up her hair because she had lice again and didn't want to give them to Annie.

"I would never intentionally harm you," Katie said. How good it would be to become angry, but there was nothing but a sense of helplessness. She was a sneaking, bloodsucking flea, slowly crushed beneath her sweet daughter's heel.

And rightly so, for I have harmed her. I am a miserable burden for Annie to bear. How embarrassed she must be.

Katie wept into her ragged sleeve.

"Take this and go." Annie held out a double florin.

Katie gazed at her daughter for a time, but the young woman would not look at her. "I'm sorry," Katie said as she took the coin and turned to walked away.

"So am I," Annie said.

Sobbing, Katie kept walking. *She has the life I wanted to her to have, and such as I am, I can't be a part of it.*

A Single Red Mitten and Twelve Pieces of White Rag

Katie and Mr. Kelly lived at Cooney's common lodging much of the time, sharing a third floor room with twenty other individuals distributed among four beds. Assuming the role of husband and wife, they signed in under the names Mary Ann Kelly and Jon Kelly. Katie had used the alias, Mary Ann, for the last two years, ever since causing a fire while drunk at Palmar's common lodging one mile to the East.

She occasionally helped in the kitchen at Cooney's, earning a little extra food for her efforts. Hung over and barely holding her own, she was washing dishes when the deputy of the common lodging, Mr. Wilkinson, passed through carrying a sack of something to the pantry. "Good morning, Mary Jane," he said, and then he was gone.

His wife, Carole, beside Katie, pulled bread from the oven. "He never knows the proper name of any woman." She set the pans on a rack to cool, then straightened and turned to Katie. "He doesn't really see women. Something wrong inside." She tapped her head. "Caught a splinter when he served in the navy. He's mistaken me for any number of women he's known, and there are times I have to convince him who I am. He squints hard at me, then something happens inside, and there I am—he knows me again."

Katie wasn't interested in pleasant conversation and remained silent. Her mouth, dry and filled with a sour, rotten taste, didn't feel as if it could form words. Wet to the elbows in greasy dishwater, she continued to scour pans with a filthy, blackened scrub brush. Her head ached with a pounding pain that accompanied each pulse of blood through the vessels in her neck.

It wants out. Katie looked at a knife among the items still to be washed. *I could use that to let the blood out and end the pain.* She picked up the blade and ran a finger along its edge. The knife was dangerously sharp, but the metal felt as if it had been sharpened with a file, nicks and burs all along its length. Scabs of flesh were stuck on it from the last joint it carved.

No, that would hurt. I'll just finish up, get some food in my belly, then go find a drink before Mr. Kelly finds me. He'd planned for them to leave London for migrant work in Kent.

"You come in at different times from Mr. Kelly," Carole said. "Aren't you afraid of the Whitechapel Murderer?"

"No," Katie said, surprised that it was the truth. Almost a week earlier, she'd read in the London Times about the victims and speculations about the killer. After what she had been through with her daughter yesterday, there hadn't been room in her head for thoughts of murders.

Then a memory recalled from the night before: As she'd stumbled drunkenly along the street, hurrying to get back to the common lodging before they locked the doors, Catherine, walking beside her, suggested she should find the Whitechapel Murderer.

What a strange thing for her to say. Did she want me to turn him in for the reward or make friends with him. Surely she doesn't want me to become his next victim.

There is so much excitement over those wretched, hapless women in the newspapers. I am like them, but nothing like that ever happens to me. No one is ever excited about me.

"Are you all right, Mary?" Carole asked.

Katie didn't respond. Finished with the dishes, she left the wash tub and sat at the table, her pounding head hung low.

Carole cut the crust off the end of one of the fresh bread loaves and gave it to her. "You don't have much to say this morning," she said.

Jon Kelly entered the kitchen, saving Katie from having to answer.

"Come, woman," he said. "We're off to Kent to go hopping. Our train leaves this afternoon. If we're going to drink more than our share, the least we can do is help pick some of the stuff. We must earn our keep."

Katie shook her head slowly.

"It'll be like a holiday." He reached for her left arm and helped her to stand. "We'll get out of London, breathe the fresh country air. It's just what you need to get clear of the doldrums."

One place is as good as another. She picked up her crust and allowed herself to be led.

~ ~ ~

And one task was as good as another. Katie picked hops for a week. Every time her basket became full, she dumped it into the big tow sacks held in wooden frameworks set at intervals along the rows of hops vines. The long rows of posts and wires supporting the climbing plants created lovely green corridors in which to work. The sun felt good on her face and when she became too hot, plenty of shade provided relief. Occasionally a laborer on stilts, a delightful sight, passed along a corridor to pick the hop cones too high for those on the ground to reach or to repair the wire and string supports. Under different circumstances, the change of landscape and fresh air would have been pleasant. But Katie suffered many aches and pains, and though an unnecessary worry, she found herself more troubled over where she'd find her next drink while so far away from all the London pubs.

She and Mr. Kelly had to wait their turn to make their meals in the communal kitchen. They also waited in line to use the outdoor toilet facilities. With Katie's urinary troubles, waiting for the toilet, then being hurried by those in line after her, became a dreadful purgatory. She and Mr. Kelly sat around the big outdoor fire pit in the evenings with the other laborers. Katie did not become drunk, though there was indeed plenty to drink. She maintained herself with doses of bitter that would not leave her unable to work the daylight hours, but were sufficient to keep her numb to most of her feelings. At night she and Mr. Kelly stayed in a hut with no furniture. They made a straw bed on the dirt floor and cuddled up close to keep warm in the night beneath blankets they had brought with them

As the week progressed, her back began to ache and she experienced abdominal cramping. Her period, which had become inconsistent in recent years, chose that most inconvenient time to return. The cramps became unbearable and the discharge voluminous, a grim, dark red. She had no hope of finding silver in it.

Her mother, like so many, called it *the blessing*. But it mocked

127

Katie. Why should she still be fertile? She thought wistfully of her children, her early life, her mother. She wondered if she would ever see Thomas again. She thought of the spot of blood on her mother's handkerchief the day she stole her thimble.

So much time had passed since her last period, she'd disposed of her menstruation needs. She asked the matron in charge of the communal kitchen if there was anything she could use to stanch the flow, and was directed to a hut with a bin full of white, wool rags.

The night before they were to return to London, Katie was unable to sleep because of her cramps. Mr. Kelly, having collected their earnings from the management and grumbling about having been cheated, had gone to bed early with a bottle. Katie stayed up late by the fire pit, drinking wine long past the time when everyone else turned in for the night. She wanted to have a smoke, but her coughing fits had been bad for the last few days and her throat was sore.

No longer tended, the fire died down, the half-burnt logs settling with graceful plumes of rising sparks and embers breaking into jumbles of orange shapes. The warmth had been stored in the stones around the pit and continued to push back the chilly night air and provide soothing heat to Katie's aching abdomen.

She found a single mitten lying in the dirt, put it on, and slipped her other hand into the pocket that held her thimble.

Catherine sat down next to her and stirred the hot coals with a stick. "*The blessing* reminds you that you have children," she said. "They love you."

"I don't even know Thomas, but I know Annie," Katie said. "She *does not* love me."

"When you go to ask her for money, she doesn't see her mother. She sees what you've become. She sees what has taken her mother away from her. But her love for you endures."

Katie wouldn't argue with her mother, but didn't share her sentiment.

"Do you see them in the embers?" Catherine said pointing. Beyond the tip of the burning stick, an orange view appeared of

Thomas consoling Annie as she wept. Thomas had grown into a man with broad shoulders and a handsome face. They stood graveside. Katie somehow knew that the coffin being lowered into a churchyard cemetery was her own. She was being buried in hallowed ground.

"She's heartbroken over the loss of her mother," Catherine said. "Once you're gone, she sees you again, she remembers the mother who loved her and filled her with fond memories, warmth, goodness."

Mum thinks I'm better off dead! Katie turned to throw harsh words at her mother, but found herself alone. Breath came in short gasps. *What does she know about it? Why should I listen to her? I have lived longer than she did and am now her senior. I'll show her she's wrong.*

Taking slower, deeper breaths restored calm. Katie returned to the hut where Mr. Kelly slept, and lay awake beside him for some time, making decisions. She would become sober and go to Annie once again. She would promise to give up drinking and find proper work. She would ask Annie to open her heart and give her another chance to prove herself worthy of love.

Tomorrow would be a new start.

On September 27, Katie awoke smiling, despite a hangover. A drink would help the throbbing pain in her head go away, but instead she would live with it. The cramps had diminished in intensity.

With a renewed sense of purpose, she tried not to think too much about the future as she stepped forward into it.

As Katie and Mr. Kelly left the hops garden and entered the road that would take them to the train station, they fell in with another couple walking in the same direction. The female was about Katie's age, tall, with thin, pale blonde hair and a wide, smiling face. The man was also tall, rail-thin, somewhat stooped and reserved.

"I'm Mary Ann Kelly," she told the woman, smiling, "and this is my husband, Jon Kelly. We're going home to London."

"I am Emily and my husband is James Birrell. We're from London too, but we're going to Cheltenham to Mr. Birrell's family."

Mr. Kelly and Mr. Birrell greeted one another, but didn't have much to say.

Katie asked Emily about her life in London, and Mr. Birrell's family.

"My husband is a dustman," Emily said, "and I char. But it has become such occasional work that even with the households we service granting us pig wash, there's never enough and the children remain hungry."

Katie was used to eating food scraps that had been left behind on the tables of patrons of pubs and taverns, then rejected by the establishments' staffs and put out for the dustman and the bone-grubber to collect. She knew when several of the public houses in Whitechapel put out their refuse and she made the rounds, sometimes competing with others for the scraps. But she knew they were relatively fresh compared to pig wash. Most households only rejected a joint or stew when it was going bad.

"We'll stay the winter with his family, and hope for better from London in the spring." Emily said.

Katie told a story about herself that left out most of what

caused her shame and suggested some stability in her life with Mr. Kelly in London. He gave her a questioning look a couple of times, but didn't interrupt. The two women made small talk for the next hour on the road. Walking in the warm sun and talking to another mother felt good. When they came to a fork in the road, the Birrells said their goodbyes and headed up the road to the right. Katie and Mr. Kelly moved to the left, but had not got far before Emily called out and ran back to Katie.

"Take these," she said, handing her two pawn tickets. "They're for a shirt and pair of boots. We shan't be back soon and it would be a waste. You should have them."

"Thank you," Katie said.

"Yes, thank you," Mr. Kelly said. He waved to Mr. Birrell, who was waiting on his wife up the lane.

When Emily was gone and Katie and Mr. Kelly resumed their trek to the train station, he said, "I haven't seen you so bright and happy for some time. It's good to have you back."

Katie's face held a smile of hope and promise.

A Black Cloth Jacket, a Chintz Skirt with Flounces and a Grey Stuff Petticoat

After paying for the train tickets, upon their return to London, Katie and Mr. Kelly had little more money than when they left to go hopping. Because they didn't have enough for both of them to have a meal and stay at Cooney's, and for Mr. Kelly to have a drink, Katie insisted that he stay at the common lodging while she went to the Mile End Casual Ward.

The superintendent at the casual ward, who knew her quite well, but whose name could not be remembered, asked where she'd been. Katie responded that she'd been hopping, and then something strange came out of her mouth: "But I've come back to earn the reward for turning in the Whitechapel Murderer. I think I know him."

Where did that come from? Was that Mum saying that?

"Mind he doesn't murder you too," the superintendent said, chuckling.

"Oh, no fear of that." Katie hid her unease with feigned mirth.

"One of the girls died last night," the superintendent said. "No family. Have a look in the clothes bin and see if there's anything you want."

Katie found a warm woolen petticoat, a chintz top skirt and an old jacket with fake fur collar and cuffs.

~ ~ ~

On September 28, when she went to Holborn to Annie's home, Katie was still sober, despite craving a drink every waking hour since leaving the hops garden. Suffering the shakes and her abdomen cramping in withdrawal, she kept her desire at bay by practicing what she would say to Annie, and imagining her daughter's positive response to her words. Having washed herself and the new clothes, she was quite presentable for the visit. She would knock on Annie's door this time. She would beg to be heard and then make the best case for herself she could. She wouldn't ask for money, merely patience.

As Katie was about to take the steps to the door of their house,

Mr. Phillips came out, followed by Annie. No doubt they had seen her approach.

Mr. Phillips hurried menacingly down the stairs. Katie had an impulse to run, but held her ground.

He came too close and leaned over her with an angry, beetling brow and balled fists. "You will not come here again."

"I shall go away, if you'll hear me out." Katie said, looking at Annie and maintaining her calm.

Her daughter remained by the door. She folded her arms before her and stared coldly.

"There is nothing you have to say we want to hear," Mr. Phillips said.

The conversation wasn't anything like what she'd imagined. Katie panicked. "I've stopped drinking," she blurted.

Annie's lips became pinched. She shook her head slowly, her eyes filled with disbelief.

"How many times have you told us that?" Mr. Phillips shouted. "We *cannot* believe you. Even if it were true, we know what you do to earn your crust. We *cannot* keep company with the likes you."

How can they know about the prostitution? The shame took the strength from her legs and back. She sagged a little, her head hung low.

Is there no way out of this life?

She pulled herself back upright, trying to look proud. Tears spilled down her cheeks. "Please," Katie cried, "you must listen to me." She looked again to Annie, but her daughter remained immobile, her eyes glistening with moisture, but still hard and impenetrable.

Annie's love is no more.

Windows opened along the street. People leaned out to get a better look at what was happening. Annie glanced up and around at her neighbors, her expression bearing the unmistakable mark of shame.

Mr. Phillips violently pulled a purse from his waistcoat, ripping the pocket as he did so. He emptied it into his right hand. He dropped the purse, grabbed Katie's hand, and hastily spilled the coins into it. "Take this and go," he said through gritted teeth. "Don't ever darken our door again." Several fell to the pavement and Katie's tear-blurred eyes reached for each and every one of the coins.

She pulled her eyes away from them to look at her daughter.

"I don't leave the house anymore for fear of meeting you," Annie said with bitterness, tears finally flowing over her cheeks. "You've killed my mother."

With that, she turned and crossed over the threshold into the house. Mr. Phillips followed her, but stopped just inside. His back still to Katie, he said, "Don't come back or you'll be sorry you did." Then he shut the door.

Katie stood alone on the street for a time weeping, periodically breaking into a great hacking cough.

She can't know what I've suffered and what it's done. Annie has nothing left for me.

The desire for drink became overpowering.

There's no way out. I can't be anyone but this drunken whore.

While the neighbors watched, she got down on her hands and knees. Mucous dripping from her mouth and nose onto the paving stones as she wept, Katie scrambled after each of the fallen coins. When she'd found them all, an amount totaling nearly two crowns, she got to her feet and fled toward the East.

Katie spent the evening in the Hoop and Grapes Pub, drinking *all sorts* and singing poorly with other drunkards and prostitutes. Desperation had introduced her to the drink several years earlier, on an occasion that it was the only thing she could afford. Before the night she'd tried it, she'd been disgusted to see it mixed over the course of an evening, with the barmaids rounding up all the drinks left on tables and the barman dumping them into a firkin and stirring it. After surviving the drink the first time, she'd allowed her imagination to work on the idea. Now, it was her way of having a bit of everything. If she concentrated, she could taste the bitter, the wine, the whiskey, and even, occasionally, a little brandy. She enjoyed one after the next and was able to ignore the small thickenings of mucous, and the bits of tobacco, ash and other debris that sometimes floated up to the top.

With Mr. Phillip's money, she could afford much better, but there was no way to know what would be needed tomorrow.

Katie sang and drank and smoked with strangers. She smiled and laughed and cavorted with the women and flirted with the men, all to suggest she was having a good time—to persuade herself—and forget what happened that day with her daughter.

Near eleven o'clock, despite her drunkenness, she gathered herself together to return to the common lodging. By the time she said her farewells, though, the clock over the bar told her she was already too late; the doors at Cooney's would be locked by the time she got there.

Leaving the pub, she thrust a hand into her pocket for the protection of her thimble, and headed for the Mile End Casual Ward. After a few paces, Catherine fell in beside her. Her mother's presence had a sobering effect that brought Katie back to memories of the experience with Annie that day. The self-pity and self-loathing returned. If that was what she got from spending time with her mother, she could do without the company.

She almost said as much, but then she was sitting with Catherine by the fire pit in the hops garden again. Her mother pointed the stick toward the jumble of orange embers. As Katie's steps continued to sound on the pavement at her feet, it became clear that she merely remembered something from several nights earlier, a part of their conversation she'd blocked out because it was too horrible.

A log settled in the pit, sending up a beautiful plume of sparks. Among the shifting embers, Katie could see an orange view of Annie sitting in a chair, being questioned in something like a courtroom.

"You know how she feels," Catherine said.

And indeed Katie did; after all, Annie was her second chance to live. She'd always been able to see the world through her daughter's eyes.

Annie had been called to identify Katie's body at the mortuary adjoining the Coroner's Court and later to answer questions at the Coroner's Inquest. The belief was that Katie had died at the hands of the Whitechapel Murderer.

She was mesmerized by the sight of her own corpse as seen through Annie's memory. Though Annie suffered pain over the loss of her mother, she'd also found much needed relief. Not relief that her mother was gone from her life. No, Annie was glad that Katie had been released from the prison emotional torment had made of her flesh.

"I *am* a burden to her," Katie said. The chill air pushed the warmth of the fire pit back, and she shivered from the cold as well as the terrible vision in the fire.

As Katie became aware again that she walked along the Whitechapel streets, she turned to her mother. "Will this truly happen?" she asked timidly, tears in her eyes.

"Yes," Catherine said.

"I'm afraid." Katie's throat tightened and words became difficult. "The mutilation…the terror."

"Look to her memories of the inquest."

When the doctor who examined Katie's body was deposed, he'd stated, "The cause of death was hemorrhage from the throat. Death must have been immediate."

"Annie shall go on to have a good life," her mother said. "She'll have a little girl named Catherine. She will call her Katie."

"When?"

"When you're willing."

Shaken and quaking in the chill night air, Katie found herself at the entrance to the casual ward. Catherine no longer stood beside her. Breathing shallowly, she struggled to compose herself. Finally, she entered, signed in, found an empty stall within one of the cells and lay in the straw bedding unable to sleep for some time.

Such as I am, I'm miserable. My life is not worth anything; not to me, nor anyone, save perhaps Jon Kelly. But he doesn't need me. He'd get along well enough. If I were not afraid, I would willingly give up my life.

What am I afraid of? Is it Hell?

Living in abject poverty had left her unable to believe in that.

No, not Hell, but perhaps the idea of my being swept up and emptied into darkness, as if by some grim dustman. Becoming nothing.... *Yet it is only the idea, here and now, that is frightening—should I become* nothing, *I shall not be aware of it...nor the darkness.*

Was it fear that she'd miss out on some good that would eventually come to her?

No, I have no worth to anyone. No one considers me deserving now.

With that thought, resentment rose in Katie, along with thoughts that she tried not to give full voice in her head. Still, they persisted, vague and doubtful at first, but with a definite theme: If she were the White Chapel Murderer's next victim, there would be sympathy. As with the first victims, the story would be everywhere in the city overnight. Her name would be on everyone's lips.

Yes, I am like those poor women who were murdered. There are many of us. As Mum would say, poor women are like the soot what falls on the city, unnoticed until it piles up and becomes a nuisance. Yes, hardly noticed...until you get a cinder in your eye!

If I were the next victim, the whole of London would be thinking about me and Conway would know.

And Annie and Mr. Phillips....

No, she would not entertain resentments toward her daughter.

Such petty, unworthy thoughts. All of it. There must be more. Have I done no good?

Yes, I helped Annie to have a good life. She knows. I sacrificed my own desires to do it....

And there was the idea...the justification, a decision pending. She touched the idea lightly, turning it to look for flaws, wanting to reject it, but knowing she would not.

I have one more sacrifice to make for Annie.

With that came a welcomed sense of relief and she slept.

~ ~ ~

The next morning, September 29, she was awakened before dawn by a disturbance in one of the other cells. Incoherent shouting resolved itself into someone clearly shouting, "*Fire!*"

Katie fled the casual ward and made her way to Cooney's to help in the kitchen. Sometimes Carole would give her a little something to drink for her hangovers in lieu of the food she normally earned for her help.

Katie knocked at the kitchen door as the sun gave an orange glow to the sky in the East. Carole answered it and let her in. Katie was given a pint of stale bitter. She donned an apron and helped Carole prepare for the morning's breakfast.

Mr. Kelly showed up early. He helped Mr. Wilkinson with a load of coal and then the two men came into the kitchen and sat down with cups of tea. While Mr. Wilkinson spoke to his wife, Katie gave Mr. Kelly the money she still had, holding back only enough for one more evening of roaring drunkenness.

"Where..." he began, his brow furrowed.

"Annie and Mr. Phillips," she whispered.

"But this is yours, then," he said, offering it back to her.

If nothing else, he is an honest man. I could have treated him better.

Unexpected tears welled up in her eyes. She pulled out her handkerchief, turned away, and pretended to sneeze to provide an excuse to be wiping her face. Turning back to him, she could see that he hadn't noticed her reaction. He still held the coins out to her. She smiled and touched his cheek gently. "You save it for me."

He grinned and nodded, put it in his pocket, and left the room.

Mr. Wilkinson raised his cup of tea to Katie and asked. "How are you this morning, Mrs. Kelly?"

"I am doing quite well," she said brightly. "Today I'll find the Whitechapel Killer and turn him in for the reward. I know who he is." Fully aware of what she meant, she said it joyfully. Catherine was right: she must find him or allow him to find her.

Mr. Wilkinson's brow rose in surprise.

Well, at least part of what I said is true. Katie winked at him.

An uncertain smile touched his lips as he sipped his tea.

Nothing

Katie spent the evening of September 29 much the way she had the night before, but did her carousing in several different pubs. By chance, she met up with Carole Wilkinson. "I were looking for a partner," Carole said. "I mean to explore the lusheries of Petticoat Lane."

"Well, I'm game," Katie said.

Carole's features took on a curious expression, and she began to laugh as she pointed to the apron around Katie's waist. "You're still wearing the flag you put on this morning!"

Katie looked down. "So I am," she said with a chuckle. She had been drinking bitter throughout the day and simply not noticed the apron. With all the layers of clothing she wore, it hardly mattered. She lifted the edge of it and curtsied.

Carole laughed, and ordered more whiskey for them both.

"I heard what you said this morning about knowing who the White Chapel Murderer is," she said.

"It's true." Katie grinned.

"Who is it, then?" Carole asked, wide-eyed.

"If I told you, you'd turn him in and I would lose out on the reward."

They both laughed. Carole thought it such a funny story, she helped Katie tell it to people in all the pubs they visited. Time passed in a blur of drunkenness as they danced with each other, rollicked with the women, and flirted with the men, laughing and joking with everyone they met.

Because the pubs had younger, prettier women, most of the men weren't interested in Katie, but that was okay. She was interested in just one man in particular. Would she recognize him when she saw him? Knowing who he was didn't matter.

By eight o'clock, having become a nuisance asking men to buy them drinks, they had managed to get themselves kicked out of The Hoop and Grapes Pub. Saying she felt ill, Carole fled home to Cooney's, while Katie remained out front, mocking the customers coming and going from the establishment. People weren't paying much attention to her, and that was fine most of the time, but not at present.

A steam-powered fire engine with bells and a whistle would get their attention. She'd seen one come screaming up the lane to put out the fire she accidentally started at Palmar's common lodging a couple years earlier.

Katie ran back and forth, up and down the street, making chugging, huffing, and puffing sounds, shouting "Clang, clang, clang," and blowing a shrill whistle between two fingers. Soon a crowd had gathered to watch. Some laughed and clapped. Some shouted "Faster, louder, before the house burns down." One fellow called out, "Quick, spray water on the fire." She figured she must be doing a good job if they knew what she imitated. She tried spitting, but it wasn't ladylike.

She laughed at the thought.

Employees and management had come out of the pub and stood with arms crossed, watching with angry eyes.

Finally, winded and dizzy, Katie's energy had run out. She slumped to the paving stones in the middle of the road. The section of pavement was smooth and fairly comfortable. She lay back and rested, closing her eyes as the crowd began to disperse.

That was all she remembered until she awoke in the Bishopsgate Police Station.

Katie sat in a chair in an office before a desk. A blurry figure sat at the desk while another stood by a window, perhaps reading something. Cells occupied the area to her right. The air held the foul odor of old fish and the flatulent smell of stewed cabbage, perhaps the remains of someone's dinner. The reek might have turned Katie's stomach if she hadn't been hungry. All she'd had to eat that night was a crust of bread scrounged from the floor of one of the pubs.

She stirred in her seat, almost falling out of it, and that attracted the attention of the one by the window. As the figure approached, it became a uniformed constable. "What is your name?" he asked.

A moment passed before she understood his words, but then Katie didn't want to answer.

"What is your name?" he asked again.

"Nothing!" she slurred.

"She's *good* for nothing in this state." He turned to the figure behind the desk. "Sir, would you help me get her into a cell?"

The man behind the desk got up and approached. He was a police sergeant. The two men helped her to stand and guided her into a cell and placed her on a wooden bench. Then they left the cell and closed the door. She curled up, using the pocket in which she carried her rags as a pillow, and fell asleep.

~ ~ ~

Katie awoke coughing, and sat up. She had no idea how long she'd been asleep.

The sounds of conversation came from beyond the bars of her cell. Her vision had improved—she could see the station's front office. A different constable, a young one with a weathered face and a short beard, stood listening to the police sergeant who sat behind the desk.

"At least the killings have brought more attention to conditions in the East End," the Sergeant said. "It breaks my heart to see women like this one." He gestured with his thumb in the direction of Katie's cell.

"A nuisance is what she is," the constable said dismissively.

The Sergeant cocked his head to one side as if trying to get a different view of the younger man. "She's probably somebody's mother."

"Not like *my* mother," the constable huffed.

"Maybe not so different," the Sergeant said slowly, giving the words an ominous tone. "Lost her husband, perhaps. Now, down and out…nobody will hire her…got nothing, no future."

"These people don't want a future, don't want to work." The younger man's response had come too quickly, and with a youthful authority that fell flat.

"So high and mighty…."

"My mother—"

"Has had a *good* life!" the sergeant said, cutting him off.

"You don't *know*."

"Nor do *you!*"

Emotions were rising, but it wasn't Katie's business. She'd heard it all before. Still, they should know she could hear them.

"So a few beggar women turn up dead. It's not unusual. They won't be missed."

"Ah, but these murders are different."

Katie began to sing softly "The Awful Execution of Charles Colin Robinson."

The policemen paused in their conversation.

The ballad was a sad song, a song of death, but somehow it filled Katie with joy. Death was not to be feared—it would be her release. She would join her mother. Perhaps she would see Charles again.

"Listen to her," the Sergeant said. "You call that a nuisance?"

"Common as soot," the young man said, dramatically brushing at the shoulders of his uniform with his hands. "*All* beggar women sing."

"Not like that, they don't," the Sergeant said.

The two men became silent for a time as she continued her song. The constable's expression softened as he became more relaxed. "It *is* a fine voice," he conceded.

A long silence descended on the station when she was finished, then the sergeant said, "Opinions are changing. All of London is looking in our direction. People don't like what they're seeing. When they get irritated enough, there'll be big changes. You wait and see. With your views, take care you're not one of those changes."

The young constable huffed. "I have my beat." He lit the lantern at his belt, took up a billy club and headed for the door.

"Careful out there," the sergeant said. He leaned back in his chair and rubbed his eyes. The younger man went out and shut the door behind him.

Katie realized she was sobering quickly. *I have to get out of here. I am willing, but I don't want to be sober.*

"Sergeant," she called, "when shall I be released?"

He turned toward her as if surprised. "When you're able to take care of yourself," he said.

"I *can* take care of myself."

He got up and moved toward her cell door and unlocked it. He stood looking at her for a time, then asked, "What is your name?"

"Mary Ann Kelly," she replied.

"Where do you live?"

"Cooney's, in Flower and Dean Street."

"All right, then." He stood aside and Katie emerged from the cell.

"Will you tell me what time it is?"

"It's one o'clock in the morning, the thirtieth of September," he said, then smiled grimly. "Too late for you to get another drink."

"Don't worry, I'll get a good hiding when I get home." The word "home" sounded strange. In the past, having a home had been important, but that time was long gone.

"And it'll serve you right," he said. "You have no right to get drunk like that at your age." He sounded stern, but there was something warm in his voice.

Katie smiled and nodded her head in agreement as he showed her the door.

"Good night old cock," she said, passing through the doorway and turning left.

"Flower and Dean is the other way," she heard him say behind her, but she kept walking. Cooney's was locked up for the night.

~ ~ ~

At random, she turned left into Houndsditch. To the left at street crossings, still close to the horizon in the distance, the one-third crescent of the moon rose between the buildings. Shrouded in foul air, it was a baleful orange.

The streets were deserted and gloomy. She would walk for a while longer and, if nothing was found, if nothing happened, she would call it a night and go to the casual ward. Her being *willing* might not produce immediate results, and she would do better with more drink in her anyway.

Katie turned right on Aldgate, then right again. As she headed into Mitre Street, an orange ember emerged from the shadows.

Quickly it became the glowing end of a cigarette or cigar, and then the silhouette of a man appeared behind it, beyond the entrance to one of the buildings. Katie turned in his direction.

He was bundled against the night air, with a scarf around his neck and lower mouth, his broad collar turned up to keep the wind off his ears and his hat pulled down low over his face.

He was *the one*. Katie wanted to flee, but instead slid her right hand into her pocket and slipped the thimble on her finger. Reaching for her mother by touching the silver inside, she found some small comfort and courage, and continued to put one foot in front of the other. When quite close, she was startled as he cleared his throat.

"I'm sorry to alarm you," he said. The voice sounded somewhat familiar.

"Not a-at all," Katie stammered, moving closer.

She coughed and took out her handkerchief to cover her mouth.

"With events of late, you'd have every right to expect one out at this hour would be up to no good," he said, "but I just needed to step out for a smoke and collect my thoughts."

"I understand. A chi-chill, dark night has a way of clearing away much of the day's troubles." Again the stammer. If she wasn't careful, she'd give herself away. But what was she trying to get away with, and why should he care?

The only light came from a swirl of mist above and behind him, making it impossible to distinguish his features.

Katie coughed again, and when she pulled the handkerchief away from her mouth, there was a spot of blood on it, almost black in the dim light.

It doesn't matter now. She put the handkerchief away.

"I take it, you have an appreciation for the dark as well," he said.

"It can be welcoming…when you're troubled." Katie struggled with the fearful hitch in her voice. "A long sleep…can do wonders…to unburden the soul."

If he knew she'd become afraid, he might attack—or he might *not* attack her. Suddenly she didn't know which she wanted.

"Don't be frightened," he said, approaching.

Katie panicked. She reached for the table knife she'd carried for so many years. In its bed ticking pocket under her top skirt, it was difficult to grasp and hung in a fold. Her hand came free from her skirt and the thimble slipped off and fell to the pavement.

Her sudden movements set him off. He moved quickly, with a flash of bright metal.

Katie stumbled back feeling only a slight pressure and then a cool breeze on her neck. Reaching for it, her hand came away with wetness.

She grew lightheaded and her legs went out from under her.

Then she lay upon the pavement, her thimble just beyond her reach. She hadn't felt any of it. She *was* being let down easily and gently to join Catherine in peace. Annie would embrace her memory. Conway would rediscover her worth.

It's just as Mum said it would be.

Her blood pooled beside her. A thread of silver spilled into it in graceful loops.

Reflected moonlight?

No. The moon…too orange and too low in the sky.

A bit of silver inside after all.

Katie was long gone before the murderer began to play.

A Body at Mortuary

Report following postmortem examination:

Female, approximately forty-five years of age. The body was on its back, the head turned to left shoulder. The arms by the side of the body as if they had fallen there. Both palms upwards, the fingers slightly bent. A thimble lay upon the pavement just beyond the second finger of the right hand. The left leg extended in a line with the body. The abdomen was exposed. Right leg bent at the thigh and knee. The throat cut across....

...She wore a black straw bonnet with green and black velvet, black beads, and black strings; a black cloth jacket trimmed with fake fur at the collar and cuffs and 2 outside pockets trimmed with black silk braid and fake fur; a chintz skirt—3 flounces with a brown button on the waistband; A worn green silk dress bodice with a black velvet collar and brown metal buttons down the front; a grey stuff petticoat with a white waistband; a very old green alpaca skirt; a very old ragged blue skirt with a red flounce and light twill lining; a white calico chemise; a man's white waistcoat with green revers; she had no drawers or stays.

Possessions:

1 thimble

1 mustard tin containing two pawn tickets: One in the name of Emily Birrell, 52 White's Row, dated August 31, 9d for a man's flannel shirt. The other is in the name of James Birrell of 6 Dorset Street and dated August 28, 2S for a pair of men's boots. Both addresses are false.

A pair of men's lace up boots with mohair laces, right boot fixed with red thread

1 red gauze silk (worn about the neck)

1 large white handkerchief

3 abalone buttons

1 blue stripe bed ticking pocket with waist band and strings

1 white-handled table knife

1 cork

2 unbleached calico pockets

1 white cotton pocket handkerchief with red and white birds-eye border

1 pair of brown ribbed stockings with white mended feet

12 pieces of white rag, slightly bloodstained

1 piece of white coarse linen

1 piece of blue and white shirting—three cornered

2 small blue bed ticking bags

1 short black clay pipe

1 tin box with tea

1 tin box with sugar

1 piece of flannel

6 pieces of soap

1 small tooth comb

1 pewter tea spoon

1 red leather cigarette case with white metal fittings

1 empty tin match box

1 piece of red flannel with pins and needles

A ball of hemp

A piece of old white apron

A printed handbill

A printed calling card for Frank Carver, 301 Bethnal Green Road

A portion of a pair of spectacles

1 red mitten

Epilogue

Conway sat in his windowless room trying to compose a ballad. Sitting and smoking his pipe, obsessively sharpening the point on his pencil with a knife, as if that might sharpen the effect of his words, he would grumble, scribble a line or two, then want to read it to Katie to get her reaction.

Since before Katie's death, nearly a month earlier, the Whitechapel murders had been a source of prodigious interest throughout the Kingdom. Because he had known her so well and for so long, he should be able to write a chapbook, with a ballad about Katie's murder that would sell many thousands of copies. While it was sad what had happened to her, there was no reason he should not capitalize on having been such a large part of her life, after supporting her for so many years. He would become rich if he succeeded.

The prose about her life had been easy enough, but the ballad had become difficult. Conway had not written a good ballad since Katie left him. He bore the burden of that as he wrote. His lines were either too distant and cold or sentimental and sweet. He couldn't strike the right balance as he shifted from anger toward her for abandoning him and destroying her life to sympathy for the warmhearted woman with the hot temper.

If she were with him, she would suggest a line or two that would pull all his efforts together into a brilliant success.

His left eye stung as he thought of the beautiful, innocent girl at her first hanging, a red silk billy around her neck.

Conway could write anything and it would sell, but couldn't allow himself to do a poor job of it. Katie deserved better and he'd have to live with it.

The stinging increased and a tear formed. The drop spilled down his cheek onto the page beneath him, blurring his words.

Am I that sentimental about my lost Katie?

No, 'tis but a cinder. He rubbed his eye and shook the

thought from his head.

Conway bent over his work fruitlessly.

About the Author

Alan M. Clark, fine arts painter, illustrator, and author, hails from Tennessee, where he grew up in a house full of human bones and old medical books. At present, he lives in Eugene, Oregon with his wife, Melody. In his 35 year freelance career, he has created illustrations for hundreds of books, including works of fiction of various genres, nonfiction, textbooks, young adult fiction, and children's books. He is the author of eighteen books, including twelve novels, a lavishly illustrated novella, four collections of fiction, and a nonfiction full-color book of his artwork. The World Fantasy Award and four Chesley Awards are among the honors he's received for his work. Mr. Clark's company, IFD Publishing, has released 45 titles in various editions that include hardcovers, paperbacks, ebooks, and audio books. IFD Publishing's authors include F. Paul Wilson, Elizabeth Engstrom, and Jeremy Robert Johnson.

www.alanmclark.com

Connect with the Author Online

You can email the author or find out more about him through the following websites:

http://www.ifdpublishing.com

http://www.smashwords.com/profile/view/IFDPublishing

IFD Publishing Paperbacks

Novels:
Of Thimble and Threat, by Alan M. Clark
Baggage Check, by Elizabeth Engstrom
Bull's Labyrinth, by Eric Witchey
The Surgeon's Mate: A Dismemoir, by Alan M. Clark
Siren Promised, by Jeremy Robert Johnson and Alan M. Clark
Say Anything but Your Prayers, by Alan M. Clark
Candyland, by Elizabeth Engstrom
Apologies to the Cat's Meat Man, by Alan M. Clark
Lizzie Borden, by Elizabeth Engstrom
A Parliament of Crows, by Alan M. Clark
Lizard Wine, by Elizabeth Engstrom
The Door that Faced West, by Alan M. Clark
The Northwoods Chronicles, by Elizabeth Engstrom
The Prostitute's Price, by Alan M. Clark
The Assassin's Coin, by John Linwood Grant
13 Miller's Court, by Alan M. Clark and John Linwood Grant
Guys Named Bob, by Elizabeth Engstrom

Collections:
Professor Witchey's Miracle Mood Cure, by Eric Witchey

Nonfiction:
How to Write a Sizzling Sex Scene, by Elizabeth Engstrom
Divorce by Grand Canyon, by Elizabeth Engstrom

IFD Publishing EBooks

(You can find the following titles at most distribution points for all ereading platforms.)

Novels:
The Prostitute's Price, by Alan M. Clark
The Assassin's Coin, by John Linwood Grant
13 Miller's Court, by Alan M. Clark and John Linwood Grant
Guys Named Bob, by Elizabeth Engstrom
Apologies to the Cat's Meat Man, by Alan M. Clark
Bull's Labyrinth, by Eric Witchey
The Surgeon's Mate: A Dismemoir, by Alan M. Clark

York's Moon, by Elizabeth Engstrom

Beyond the Serpent's Heart, by Eric Witchey

Lizzie Borden, by Elizabeth Engstrom

A Parliament of Crows, by Alan M. Clark

Lizard Wine, by Elizabeth Engstrom

Northwoods Chronicles, by Elizabeth Engstrom

Siren Promised, by Alan M. Clark and Jeremy Robert Johnson

To Kill a Common Loon, by Mitch Luckett

The Man in the Loon, by Mitch Luckett

Jack the Ripper Victim Series: Of Thimble and Threat by Alan M. Clark

Jack the Ripper Victim Series: The Double Event (includes two novels from the series: *Of Thimble and Threat* and *Say Anything But Your Prayers*) by Alan M. Clark

Candyland, by Elizabeth Engstrom

The Blood of Father Time: Book 1, The New Cut, by Alan M. Clark, Stephen C. Merritt & Lorelei Shannon

The Blood of Father Time: Book 2, The Mystic Clan's Grand Plot, by Alan M. Clark, Stephen C. Merritt & Lorelei Shannon

How I Met My Alien Bitch Lover: Book 1 from the Sunny World Inquisition Daily Letter Archives, by Eric Witchey

Baggage Check, by Elizabeth Engstrom

D. D. Murphy, Secret Policeman, by Alan M. Clark and Elizabeth Massie

Black Leather, by Elizabeth Engstrom

Novelettes:

The Tao of Flynn, by Eric Witchey

To Build a Boat, Listen to Trees, by Eric Witchey

Children's Illustrated:

The Christmas Thingy, by F. Paul Wilson. Illustrated by Alan M. Clark

Collections:

Suspicions, by Elizabeth Engstrom

Professor Witchey's Miracle Mood Cure, by Eric Witchey

Short Fiction:

"Brittle Bones and Old Rope," by Alan M. Clark

"Crosley," by Elizabeth Engstrom

"The Apple Sniper," by Eric Witchey

Nonfiction:

How to Write a Sizzling Sex Scene, by Elizabeth Engstrom

Divorce by Grand Canyon, by Elizabeth Engstrom

IFD Publishing Audio Books

Novels:

The Door That Faced West by Alan M. Clark, read by Charles Hinckley

Jack the Ripper Victim Series: Of Thimble and Threat, by Alan M. Clark, read by Alicia Rose

Jack the Ripper Victim Series: Say Anything But Your Prayers, by Alan M. Clark, read by Alicia Rose

Jack the Ripper Victim Series: The Double Event by Alan M. Clark, read by Alicia Rose (includes two novels from the series: *Of Thimble and Threat* and *Say Anything But Your Prayers*)

A Parliament of Crows by Alan M. Clark, read by Laura Jennings

A Brutal Chill in August by Alan M. Clark, read by Alicia Rose

The Surgeon's Mate: A Dismemoir, by Alan M. Clark, read by Alan M. Clark

Apologies to the Cat's Meat Man, by Alan M. Clark, read by Alicia Rose

The Prostitute's Price, by Alan M. Clark, read by Alicia Rose

The Assassin's Coin, by John Linwood Grant, read by Alicia Rose

13 Miller's Court, by Alan M. Clark and John Linwood Grant, read by Alicia Rose